BET YOU

FRANKLIN U #4

NEVE WILDER

Copyright © 2022 by Neve Wilder

All rights reserved.

Beta Reading: Janine Cloud

Editing By: One Love Editing

Proofing: Charity VanHuss

Cover Design: Natasha Snow Designs

Cover photo: Xram Ragde

This book is a work of fiction. Names, characters, places, and incidents are products of the author's imagination, or are used fictitiously.

References to real people, events, organizations, establishments, or locations are intended to provide a sense of authenticity and are used fictitiously. Any resemblance to actual events, locations, organizations, or persons living or dead, is entirely coincidental.

All song titles, songs, and lyrics mentioned in the novel are the property of the respective songwriters and copyright holders.

All rights reserved.

No part of this book may be reproduced in any form or by any electronic or mechanical means, including information storage and retrieval systems, without written permission from the author, except for the use of brief quotations in a book review.

Wilder Press monitors international sites for infringing material. If infringement is found (illegal downloading or uploading of works), legal action will be taken.

ABOUT THIS BOOK

Spencer

Whose brilliant idea was it to build university housing next to one of Franklin U's most notorious party frats?

I'm a real student—the kind who actually came to college to *learn*, not some dumb frat bro who sees Franklin U as a four-year challenge to consume the most booze and throw out the best pick-up line.

Their all-hours lifestyle is driving me crazy. Not to mention, the jerks keep taking my assigned parking spot.

But the worst offender might be Cory Ingram. Sure, he has a smile that could melt a polar ice cap, but no way will I ever be one of his minions. I'm pretty sure I made that clear when I blew my top at him. So I have no idea why he's suddenly everywhere around me, turning on the charm like I might actually fall for it.

Nope. Not gonna happen.

Cory

From the first day I set foot on Franklin U's campus, everything has been golden. I have a ton of friends, endless parties to be the life of, and whoever I want in my bed on any given night.

Sure, I'm a shameless party boy, but I'm not a jerk. Ask anyone. Seriously.

Even the crotchety old groundskeeper waves and smiles at me when I pass.

Then there's Spencer Crowe. I've never seen a guy's face get so red over a parking spot. Even when I try to make it right, he proceeds to give me the tongue-lashing of a lifetime—which is about the moment I notice that, in addition to being irrationally irate, he's also crazy hot.

My friends think I've finally met the one person I can't seduce...

Bet you I can.

AUTHOR'S NOTE

These FUKing books are total standalones and you don't need to have read the others to enjoy this one (though you should, because they're awesome).

If you are following the recommended reading order, the timeline of this one intersects with *The Glow Up*, *Learning Curve*, and *Making Waves*. None of the couples in those books are together... yet. Happy reading!

1

SPENCER

I swear to god, I'm gonna...
I growl at the parking space before me. The one currently occupied by a car that's decidedly not mine. I know that because a. I am presently sitting at the wheel of my un-chic but reliable Toyota Corolla, hands tightening on the cracking leather as I seethe at my windshield and b. not in a million years of fever dreams could I ever afford the shiny army green Jeep Wrangler so casually occupying the slot that had been designated as mine at the start of the semester three weeks ago.

Sleek, gleaming, and with the top removed, it speaks of carefree southern California afternoons, of drives filled with salty breezes to riffle one's hair. Of a driver who actually has the time and luxury to do those things rather than cramming in as many shifts at Franklin U's favorite student haunt, Shenanigans, as humanly possible and studying until God-save-us-all o'clock in the morning. The faded COEXIST sticker on the back bumper strikes me as particularly ironic because right now, I want nothing more than to gun my little car forward and dent the bumper in.

Coexist like that, stupid Jeep.

I know better, though. Criminal charges aside, my Corolla will inevitably suffer more than the rugged Jeep.

I still harbor an instantaneous and fierce dislike for the owner of the Jeep, though, whoever he might be.

This is the fourth time someone has taken my spot, and though it's always a different car, I know the collective culprits.

My gaze swings to the Delta Iota Kappa frat house (aka DIK house) to the left, the parking lot jam-packed with similar examples of affluence in a variety of appealing colors. Last week, it had been a Porsche the same color of the nearby ocean I rarely get to enjoy that had taken my spot. Before that, an Audi with a custom job the color of a sunset—something I also haven't gotten to enjoy in forever. And yeah, my assigned spot is literally right next to the edge of their lot, but no way they didn't know. They just don't care.

Because they're frat dudes, and as long as they have their brotherhood, booze, and an occasional fundraiser to reassure themselves that they're giving back to the community, they never do.

A couple of Solo cups shift in the breeze and roll onto the nearby lawn of the Life Sciences Living and Learning (LaL house for short, though it's been further nicknamed the LoL house by the DIKs next door, who apparently find a whole house of people devoted to sciences that might save the earth and their garish automobiles somehow hilarious).

I'd been dying to get into the house since I'd learned about it freshman year. Eleven fellow ecology, biology, and zoology geeks living together and sharing knowledge? Sign me up. That's my kind of fraternity and the quintessence of the word, not some dumb social custom for the rich or a perpetual excuse to party and be a tool.

But after three weeks of drowning out the DIK's constant parties with earplugs, tripping over Solo cups and random shoes

—seriously, why is there only ever one shoe? Do people not notice the exact moment they lose a shoe?—and dealing with parking issues, I'm starting to question the wisdom of my decision. My friend, Liam, warned me. I didn't listen.

Ugh.

I heave another sigh that echoes the sound of my AC as it shudders, then back the car up and pull down the street in the opposite direction. I don't have time to fight this battle today.

I'm sweating by the time I punch in the code at the front door of the LaL house. I have just enough time to grab a quick shower before heading over to Shenanigans for my shift as a server. Glamorous? No, but it's fairly mindless work, and management is flexible with student schedules, which is key.

A few housemates are scattered around the living room in front of the TV as I walk in.

My best friend, Darby, a zoology major, finger guns me as I nudge the door closed with my heel, my backpack and laundry bag slung over one shoulder. There's a single washer and dryer on the premises, but it's always in use, and once I discovered a laundromat a couple of miles away, I started going there instead and using the time to study. It gets me off campus and out of my usual routine for a while.

"I finished my She-Ra armbands," she says. "You'll have to come see later. Sure I can't convince you to try He-Man?"

I bark out a laugh. "Sure, check back with me in six months after I've dropped out of school and become a gym rat for six hours a day." Right now, that doesn't sound so bad, actually.

"I've got that friend in theatrical makeup. He could make you a whole set of pecs, probably."

"Pass," I tell her. I know my limits with cosplay, and beefcake heroes are beyond them.

"Finnnne." She frowns, grabbing my arm as I start to pass. "Why the storm cloud face? Is Ted being weird again?"

I am maybe a little too attached to my crowntail betta, but whatever. It's better than being attached to booze or drugs. Ever since I moved into the LaL house, he's been slightly off. I blame the noise and lights from next door, which are far more disruptive than your average dorm. "He's still adjusting. I've been thinking of getting him some friends." When Darby chuckles, I flip her the bird. "I've gotta motor. Some dumbass frat guy parked in my spot, again, and I had to park all the way over on Lee."

"Again? You should definitely go talk to them."

"I know. But I don't have time today." Plus, I dread walking over there and having to approach a bunch of meatheads who will probably think it's hilarious that the dork next door is pissed about his parking spot.

"In the meantime, consider it free exercise. You'll be my He-Man in no time," she chimes after me as I hoof it up the stairs.

Right.

My room is on the second floor of the house and shares a hall bath with two other guys. Darby and Selena share a bath, and then there are a couple of larger baths split between housemates. The hot water situation gets a little dicey sometimes, but overall, the space and housemates are way better than the dorms I'd occupied the prior two years, so I've been trying my best to overlook the noise from the frat house, along with the view of its stucco facade out my two windows. I've never been to New York City, but I've heard people there get used to sleeping through the constant blare of sirens and horns. Surely I'll eventually get used to Dua Lipa at 3:00 a.m.

After showering, I check on Ted. He's definitely not as active as he used to be this time of day. I give him a little food and watch him dart to the top of the tank to nibble on it before letting himself sink back to the gravel at the bottom. "I'm going to get you some tank mates," I tell him. "This isn't healthy. I think you're lonely." I might as well be talking to myself. Technically, I *am* talking to myself.

Except I'm not lonely. Am I? I grab my Shenanigans uniform from the back of the chair where I've laid it out for maximum efficiency and do a quick self-check as I pull it on, hearing my mom's voice in the back of my mind. HALT. Hungry. Angry. Lonely. Tired. The four horsemen of foul moods. My mom is a licensed counselor back in Nacogdoches, Texas, where I was born and raised and is constantly on me about monitoring my stress levels. And, okay, I am currently three out of the four horsemen. But I'm not sure about lonely. I've got plenty of friends, and I hooked up with a guy off an app a week ago. No, wait, make that three months ago. But that's really all I have time for at the moment. Still, it's kind of shocking and a little scary to realize how quickly three months have passed.

Deciding I'm doing well enough, I jet back downstairs, toss a quick wave to my housemates, and book it out the door.

My gangly, completely unathletic jog skids to a halt at the guy digging keys from his pocket next to the Jeep parked in my space.

When he glances up, my breath catches in my throat, even as irritation needles through me. Almost everyone at FU knows Cory Ingram, if not by name, then by reputation. His parents own a huge advertising firm with offices all over California, in New York City, Minneapolis, and Boston. A wing of the communication arts building bears their family name, and I know all about this because my freshman-year roommate, a graphic design major, developed a huge unrequited crush on Cory during a communications class they shared. I'll grant Cory is incredibly attractive. As in, have you ever looked at someone and found them so attractive that it seemed improbable? His chestnut curls are the perfect embodiment of casually windswept, and his face is the perfect combination of high cheekbones, a ridiculously carved jawline, and kissable lips that should only exist on marble museum statues but have miraculously come together on a living, breathing human being. That kind of improbable.

I'm aware that looks are subjective, but plenty of people must also agree with me because Cory is a notorious player. He doesn't even do anything special. He's not one of FU's sports gods like Tyson Langley or Peyton Miller, just another wealthy guy among plenty on campus.

And apparently, he's also the frat guy who's parked in my space, just because he could.

Figures.

"Hey, man." He upnods me with a casual, cool-as-can-be smile, warm brown eyes sparkling like he doesn't have a care in the world. Entitled bastard. I know that smile is meant to be disarming, but it's not gonna work on me.

I scowl at him. "I'm not sure you're aware, but there's something wrong with your car."

His brows shoot up dramatically. "Shit, there is?"

He takes a step back and scans the Jeep's chassis, the concern etched in his perfectly thick brows causing a tiny twinge of schadenfreude in me. Apparently, there are some things he cares about.

"Mm-hmm. See, it's in my spot. And that's not the first time that's happened, *man*. It's the fourth time in two weeks."

"Oh, shit. But..." His concern morphs into a thoughtful frown. "I'm pretty sure this is the first time I've parked here. Our lot was full, and—"

"Right, so you decided you'd just take my spot."

"I wasn't going to be long. Again, I'm sorry. I'll move it."

"Really? No, I don't think you're sorry. I think that like every other time this has happened before, you and your fellow entitled frat bros think, 'Oh, no biggie, I'll just park in front of the geek house and steal one of their spots—'"

Cory's annoyingly square jaw slackens. "Dude, I think you're being a little harsh. I've hardly ever seen anyone in this space. We thought it was just an extra one."

I stare at him. My car is in this spot frequently since campus and the surrounding area are highly walkable. "You rarely ever see anyone in the space because you don't pay attention, and because I work a fucking lot paying to go to school here and live in this house, and I have places to go and errands to run." I'm getting derailed, but I can't seem to stop myself. "A foreign concept for you, I'm sure. But I do that so I can afford to know this one spot in particular is mine, and when I'm dead on my feet, I can think to myself, 'At least finding a parking spot when I go home is one thing I don't have to worry about.' Except—" I gesture toward the frat house. "—then I come rushing home so I won't be late for my next shift and find, once again, my spot has been taken. Then I have to go ease my car into the only free spot a quarter mile away on Lee Street next to a dumpster, run home, shower, and then run back to my car so I can deposit a check before I start said shift, where I will probably arrive smelling like said dumpster."

Cory cocks his head. "Don't you think you're blowing this a little—"

Probably. "No!" I cut him off, impatient. "I'm not blowing anything!" My diatribe comes to an awkward halt as I realize how wrong that sounds. Cory's lips twitch at the corners, suggesting he's picked up on it, too.

"Whoa, whoa." He puts his hands up. "I didn't ask you to blow anything. Yet." The humor dancing in his eyes makes me even more irritated.

I'm irritated that I'm being more aggressive than I usually would because after that not-so-subtle innuendo, I have to fight not to look down at his crotch, not to find the amusement in his tone actually kind of disarming. Even that flirty twist of a smile on his lips is enough to put my body on high alert against an unintentional boner. I don't mess with guys like Cory, though. I decide I must be all four horsemen after all. Unacknowledged loneliness is a damn sneaky bitch.

"You're clearly not appreciating the gravity of this situation," I tell him.

Cory's smile widens. That can't be good.

2

CORY

Damn, this dude is fired up. And while I hear the words coming out of his mouth, it's the visuals that strike me. Dark brown hair swept back from his forehead in a way that catches the sunlight in threads of warm gold. His eyes are a crystalline blue and what I'd consider penetrating if they weren't filled with so much fury that I'm convinced he's trying to laser me to ash on the spot. And a mouth that, well, if it wasn't currently spewing venom at me, would leave me curious about how it'd feel wrapped around my cock.

How have I not noticed this guy before?

Or have I?

Shit, have I slept with him?

Maybe that's why he's so pissed over a parking spot? Who the hell gets this butthurt over a parking spot without some background motivation? I mean, I'm always up-front with my hookups that I am in no way relationship material, but that doesn't mean feelings don't get hurt sometimes. Maybe this guy is a ghost from hookups past?

"Have I slept with you?" I blurt, interrupting him while he's saying something again about a dumpster on Lee Street.

His jaw snaps shut, then opens, bewilderment wrinkling his forehead. "What? Of course not," he growls as if I've mortally offended him by the suggestion, which in turn kinda offends me.

Look, my body count is pretty high, but like I said, I'm always up-front with my partners, always get consent, and am dedicated to their pleasure as much as mine. I mean, Jesus, I once went down on a girl for two hours because she'd never had an orgasm from oral before, and it took us that long to figure out what combination of lips, tongue, and fingers was the winning ticket.

But by god, we fucking found it. And then celebrated after with a two-hour nap before she blew me a kiss as she left. I never heard from her again, but I like to think she's out and about these days tugging the roots of guys' hair as they bring her to multiple orgasms.

God, he's still going. I zero in on his mouth, the plump Cupid's bow and the thinner lower lip—which gives him a stern look that's really working for me.

I shake my head, trying to focus on the words coming from those sexy lips.

"...not if you were the last man alive."

Okay, so he's gay. Or bi. I squint at him, still confused. "I'm sorry, but I need to ask again: Is this amount of aggression really warranted over a parking space?" When he purses his lips, I can't help it—I have to fight back a grin. It's just... he's so fucking indignant. "Look, I've said I'm sorry about your space, and I'm moving the car now."

"Which would only help me if I could time travel back to an hour ago to before you parked in the spot."

"How about I drive you to your car?" I figure that's a considerate offer and the best proverbial olive branch that I can think of at the moment.

He blinks in surprise before his mouth pulls into another

scowl. "No, thanks. I'll walk." He stalks past me and starts down the street.

I shrug and throw my hands up. I've done all I can do, I decide, so I climb into my Jeep and crank it. A glance over my shoulder shows him still marching down the road, looking like a pissed-off parking attendant. He's got nice legs, though. And an ass that fills out his faded blue shorts nicely. Does he work out? Surely I would've seen him in the gym at some point, though, unless he goes super early. It's still bothering me that I can't pin him one way or another, given that I'm an established social butterfly.

I back out of the space and start to head in the other direction to avoid him, then decide fuck it. I'm not really a dick, but I dunno, thinking back on everything he's said gets under my skin, too, so what's the harm in heckling him a little?

I slow to a crawl when I get closer and paste on a megawatt smile as I creep beside him.

He glances over, lips curling into something that closely resembles the snarl my dog Minnie would give our other dog, Frodo, when he'd get too close to her food. Fuck, it's kinda growing on me. I wonder what he looks like when he smiles.

"Sure you don't want a ride?" I drawl. "We're going the same direction anyway."

He flips me off. "I'd probably catch something from your car seat."

"Maybe some cool quotient or a couple of envious glances." I smirk.

He shakes his head. "Scratch that. Your ego takes up the rest of the space."

"You can sit in its lap. It won't mind, I'm sure." Probably the worst moment to try to flirt with him, and his unchanging expression supports that theory.

"Jeez, just go on." He waves me off, and I can't help the

chuckle that bubbles up in my chest. It's just so rare that someone actually dislikes me that I don't even know what to do with it. But still, sensing I've probably pushed him to his limit, I toss him a wave and a "see you around" as I gun the engine and speed off, barely catching what is likely an "I hope not" as I go.

"Ingrammmmmmm. Over here," Will Royer, one of my frat brothers, shouts as I mosey into Shenanigans a few hours later. I've finished my classes for the day, played a few rounds of disc golf, and now I'm ready for an icy-cold beer with my bros.

I head in his direction, tossing waves and greetings as I go. I fucking love this place. I'd be a lifelong student if I could, anything to keep me out of a frigid office in my parents' New York firm, which is waiting on me when I graduate. They built the firm from the ground up into one of the top agencies in the US, and they're both quintessential go-getters, which I respect the hell out of. And, as their only son, they both have strong opinions on what I do with my life. Read: continue the family legacy of brilliance in advertising. Having grown up around it, it's an easy career path for me. I'm good at it, I like people, and also, it's hard to make a career out of sailing tourists around the coast, no matter how much I prefer the outdoors over the idea of being stuck in an office all day. I can sail on weekends—at least that's what I tell myself, blithely ignoring the full weekends my folks usually put in at the agency or prepping for meetings, and that NYC is stupid cold for six months out of the year, unlike Cali.

I drop into a chair next to Royer, and he passes me a beer that I suck down gratefully.

"How was disc golf?" he asks.

"Solid. We missed you, though. Jackson can't toss for shit. Made for a long game." I like my gym time, but I've sucked at most traditional dude sports, like football, my entire life. Throwing a Frisbee, casting a line, or bench-pressing 210 pounds is the extent of my athletic capabilities.

"I'll be there next time," Royer says distractedly as he eyes another table. I vaguely recognize the girl he's checking out.

I cast a glance around, surveying the crowd, too. I'm in the mood to hook up tonight. My gaze lands on a table toward the back, where I ping-pong between a blonde with a ponytail and a reddish-golden-haired guy, trying to discern if they're together, so I miss the server's approach until he's right there staring down at me.

Parking Spot Guy, name unknown. Scowl all too familiar. But a second later, he plasters on a smile and addresses Royer. "Want another beer? Any food?" His gaze swings toward me, smile tinged with acid. "How about you? Beer? You do have to actually pay for it, though. You can't just help yourself to it like, say, someone else's parking spot."

Here we go again. I smile at him as I reach over, snag Royer's half-full beer, and help myself to a long gulp. Royer tries to smack my hand away with a cursing protest, but I'm too quick.

"Mmmm. Other people's stuff is just *so* tasty." I wipe the back of my mouth with my hand and return the beer to the table.

Something flashes behind Parking Spot's eyes, even as a tendril of heat sizzles through my gut for the unintended innuendo. It's evident Parking Spot caught it, too. He narrows his eyes. "I'll give you a minute to look over the menu."

"Nah, I know what I want. I'll take a Dos Equis and some loaded nachos."

"Nachos. Got it. As in, nacho parking spot." He shoves his pen back in his pocket and arches a brow, somehow managing to remain serious as he lobs out what has to be the worst dad joke in my entire twenty-one years.

"Jokes are nacho forte, my friend." I finger gun him with a wink.

"I'm definitely nacho friend," he claps back.

Royer groans as Parking Spot Guy spins on his heel and walks off. "What's going on here? How did I land in nacho pun hell. Do you know that guy?"

"Not really. He lives in the LoL house next door and went off on me earlier for parking in his spot."

"Seems a little harsh over a parking spot."

"That's exactly what I said." I knew I was right. "According to him, it happens frequently. But I've only parked in it once."

"That space right on the edge of our lot?"

"Yep."

Royer cackles. "I've definitely parked in it before. One of us should snag it again tonight. I'll bet his shift goes late."

My instinct is to agree, but a pang of guilt hits me when I think about him railing on me earlier about busting his ass to get to work, and working on top of classes—something I've never had to do. I imagine him getting home exhausted at 2:00 a.m. and wanting nothing more than to collapse in bed, then seeing someone has taken his parking spot again. Yeah, nope. Even I'm not that big of an asshole.

For now.

I wave Royer off. "It's cool. He has a point. We have enough spots if a few of the brothers would stop parking like jerks and actually look at the lines."

Royer squints at me. "Huh, you must want to bang him. Hate to break it to you, man, but he puts out nothing but 'fuck you' vibes when he's looking at you."

I shrug. I find him attractive, yeah, but I've not considered hooking up with him. However, Royer's comment piques my competitive side. "I think I could get him in bed."

"Maybe with a roofie or a disguise."

I slug him in the arm. "Nope, just my charm." I'm not actually sure I could, but I do like a challenge, and this guy would definitely be a challenge. "Might take me a hot minute, though."

"I'm not gonna hold my breath."

3

SPENCER

Gwen lets me clock out at midnight, which is great timing since I'm about to keel over. Cory and his friends hung around until almost 11:30, and all the interaction with him got my adrenaline pumping. Now comes the inevitable crash.

Luckily, my class tomorrow isn't until 10:00, so I'll be able to sleep in a little and still get all of my homework done before I have to go.

I drive home in a daze, my heart rate speeding up as I close in on the LaL house. I swear to god, if someone's in my space again—especially Cory, because that seems like something he would do—I'm gonna egg his Jeep and double-park behind it. I really will.

But somewhat surprisingly, the space is empty. Also surprising is the tiny twinge of... I don't even know what, I feel. I mean, it's not like I want to have any further encounters with Cory Ingram. Two in one day is enough for a lifetime.

I brush it off as exhaustion and climb out of the car.

The interior of the house is quiet, only Selena and Chance zoned out on the couch when I get inside. I give them a tired hello before heading upstairs.

Unfortunately, the quiet isn't universal. Once in my bedroom, the thumping bass from late night at DIK house is pervasive, interrupted by an occasional shout or whoop. Liam warned me, to be fair, and usually, some earplugs solve the issue. Usually.

Because once I'm lying in bed, ears stuffed with foam, I struggle to sleep. I keep thinking back to my encounter with Cory this afternoon and then again at Shenanigans. How can a person go multiple years without interacting with another, and then suddenly, they're everywhere?

I toss and turn for a while, then give up and fold my arms behind my head, watching Ted swim back and forth in his tank. Sometimes that's enough to send me off, but tonight, I find myself analyzing his movements, trying to decide if he seems more agitated than normal. Inconclusive, but I'm definitely going to move forward with getting him some tank mates.

A muted green-blue glow draws my eye to the blinds covering my window. They're cheap and old, a couple of the slats dented or angled funny from wear and tear and bracketed on either side by some navy curtains someone left behind last year.

I watch the shifting light, puzzling over it. Does some DIK have a disco ball in their room? I snort. I wouldn't be surprised. Seems like a DIK-ish thing to do. There are no other colors, though, and it doesn't flash the way a disco ball would, thank fuck. I really would consider going over there if that were the case.

Sheer curiosity pulls me out of bed toward the window, where I nudge one of the slats that's come completely off the strings on one end so I can peek through at the side of the frat house about twenty feet away. There are a few windows scattered over its edifice that I've never paid much attention to, some of them dark, one with light peeking beyond curtains pulled tightly across it. The blue-green light emanates from a double window directly across and a tiny bit below mine.

Pulling the blinds down farther, I scope it out. It's some sort of light-projection machine that fills the room with a soothing kaleidoscope of cerulean and emerald and makes me think of currents moving through the ocean. It's pretty cool, actually. Maybe I could get one. I'll bet Ted would like it. I'm making a mental note to search on Amazon tomorrow and see how expensive something like that is when movement stops me in my tracks.

There's just enough light for me to discern two guys, one slightly taller than the other, pressed together, kissing, running their hands over each other. Their clothes are still on and... jeez, it's been a while since I've touched or been touched like that. Just watching them has my cock hardening wistfully.

The taller guy yanks his shirt off while the shorter guy trails kisses down the guy's chest, slowly lowering to his knees. Light washes over the taller guy's skin, bathing angular features in soft hues. I catch a peek of a tattoo on his bicep and follow the swirling glow up to his face.

Of all the fucking luck. It's Cory.

My parking-spot nemesis is the tall, gorgeously muscled, head-thrown-back-in-pleasure, sexy plump-lips-parted guy I'm staring at like a lech.

I let go of the blinds and stumble backward, air whooshing in and out of my lungs rapidly. This is creepy of me, right? It's creepy to watch someone else hooking up. It's creepier still that it's Cory. Where the fuck are the blinds on the window anyway? Why's it just wide open like that for pent-up guys like me to look in on?

I turn to go back to bed and stop. As if my feet are now conspirators with my throbbing dick, they won't move forward. Maybe the guy's an exhibitionist. Maybe he just doesn't care. If he's getting it on in front of a window with no coverings on it, is it really so bad if I keep looking? I might not like Cory, but I can appreciate a hot body and a hot show.

Besides, he parked in my spot earlier, which is a violation in and of itself. Is it really so bad that I do sort of similar? He should have pulled his curtains or blinds.

Spinning back around, I edge forward and peer through the blinds once more, an envious groan escaping me as the guy on his knees rests back on his heels and wraps a hand around Cory's cock, stroking it slowly. Cory sinks a hand into the guy's hair and pulls him up after a few moments. Another lingering kiss is exchanged. They're clearly enjoying themselves, and heat ripples through my gut as I reach inside my pajama pants and caress my aching dick. I so shouldn't be doing this, but I'm not sure I can stop now, especially when Cory surprises the hell out of me by pushing down the other guy's shorts and dropping to his knees.

Knowing what little I do of Cory, I pegged him as the type to make his partner do all the work before he fucked them and discarded them, but Cory licks and sucks this other guy's dick sensually, lapping at it like he's enjoying every second. The hot feeling sizzles through me again with an added sharpness of envy. I miss connection like that and intimacy.

The other guy's face, what I can make out of it, is strained and rapturous, like Cory working him over is the best thing he's ever had. And damn, maybe it is.

I squeeze my shaft, a shudder of pleasure rolling through me as Cory picks up the pace. The other guy is definitely moaning. Is Cory? God, I wonder what he sounds like. I think about his booming voice earlier, the amused yet slightly bewildered spark in his eyes. Would it be there still if he was on his knees in front of me? I shouldn't even entertain the thought because that's never gonna happen, but my dick doesn't care.

Pleasure mounts and throbs low in the base of my spine, and I have to back off when the other guy pushes Cory away and onto his back right there in the middle of the floor like they can't be bothered with a bed. They roll and wrestle for dominance, and suddenly, Cory's back is to me as he sinks between the other guy's knees and thrusts against him. Cory's ass is perfect, of course. Round and hard and powerful as it flexes and contracts with motion. I imagine grabbing it, holding it, tugging him closer, pulling him deeper inside me, and feeling every one of his thrusts like a shock wave as his jaw tightens with desire, his eyes dark and hot upon me.

My orgasm sneaks up on me as I stroke harder, faster, teeth sinking into my lower lip, breath coming in gusty gasps that break in sweet relief when it crests. It roars through me, one of the best solo orgasms I've had since I can remember, and I drift on the aftershocks bathing my body in a warm glow, momentarily forgetting I've just jerked off to a guy whose Jeep I strongly considered egging earlier.

When I blink my eyes open, Cory has gone still on top of the other guy, whose arms are wrapped around him. Then Cory rolls off beside him. They laugh, and I consider whether I might be able to get off again whenever they resume their activities and one of them fucks the other, because surely that's where this is going.

But after a few more moments of peeking through the blinds in between cleaning myself up, it becomes clear that's not going to happen. Cory rolls to his feet and helps the guy up. They chat as the other guy pulls his clothes on, and then, with a brief kiss, the other guy departs.

That's it?

That's fucking it?

One of FU's most notorious players—and there are a few—

has just sent a guy off after humping him in the middle of his floor?

A weird mix of relief and disappointment rings through me as Cory shuts the door. He picks his clothes up from the floor and tosses them onto the back of a desk chair, then just sort of stands in the middle of the room zoning out, I guess, fingers of one hand stroking over the other forearm idly, moving up until it reaches his bicep, where it lingers, caressing gently.

Then he snaps into action, walking over to the desk. The room goes dark a second later, and I can just make him out as he walks toward his bed and collapses onto it.

My breath leaves in a rush, and the strange cocktail of adrenaline, postorgasmic endorphins, and warring feelings over what I've seen and who was in the starring role lingers as I crawl into bed and shut my eyes.

4

CORY

Buffet breakfasts in the DIK house dining room are a zoo on weekday mornings.

I'm immediately assaulted by a pancake frisbeed in my direction as I shuffle in, raking a hand through my hair drowsily.

Jason, one of my pledgemates, grins as I catch it sliding down the side of my face and take a bite of it. Tasty.

"Guess all that disc golf is good for something," he chuckles.

"Touché." I help myself to the spread laid out and carry my plate to a table, plopping down next to Royer.

"Good rest of the night?" Royer gives me a knowing smirk as a couple of brothers pause what they're doing to glance over. I've had some epic stories before, and I'm generous about sharing my adventures here and there without giving out names of my partners.

I seesaw my hand. "Decent." Then I realize it may sound like I'm throwing shade on my hookup. Pete? Yeah, Pete. "Dude was cool, just... I don't know. Wasn't feeling it as much as I thought I was." I couldn't pinpoint it exactly because I'd been horny as fuck earlier in the night when we were at Shenanigans and also in the mood to top. Pete had definitely been down, but once we got back to my room and started fooling around, my enthusiasm had waned. I sent him off after a half-hearted frot session, but at least he got off.

Javi chuckles. "Someone better check your temp."

"Where's the rectal thermometer?" Royer twists in his seat to call back to Finn, "Don't put a mark on Ingram's leaderboard. He choked." According to campus legend, DIK house has a secret room containing a scoreboard of every member's sexual encounters. It's a bunch of bullshit, but when I was a freshman, our president at the time attempted a campaign to set the record straight, and it didn't take. At this point, we just embrace it. It's mostly amusing, though sometimes annoying, like the time one of my hookups insisted repeatedly I put his name on my "score sheet" and followed up with multiple texts daily until I finally told him I would just to pacify him. He was an odd duck.

"I didn't choke." I snort defensively. "I never choke."

"Ingram choked, duly noted," Royer says with finality and a rakish grin. "There's a first."

With my failure to launch last night at the front of my mind, I swallow a bite of eggs and level a stare on him. "Our server last night," I start, and he lifts a brow. "You really don't think I could get him in bed?"

"Which server?" Javi leans around Royer with interest.

"Spencer. A little shorter than me, dark hair. Perpetually frustrated." I may have taken the time to look at the credit card receipt since the irate little hottie hadn't bothered to introduce himself in the midst of yelling at me or subsequently trying to ignore me at Shenanigans. Then, even more rudely, he kept popping up in my head the rest of the night, the drawn set of his sexy-ass mouth and scornful pull of his brows taunting me.

"Hard sell, yeah. I have serious doubts." Royer shrugs, but Javi's eyes flash with mischief. He knows I have trouble backing down from a challenge. As in, I never have, even when it led to me almost getting arrested after streaking a lacrosse game freshman year. Thank goodness for masks and sprint training.

"I can win him over," I insist.

"Yeah?" Javi chuckles. "What do you want to put on it?"

"Ummm, I win and you all cover food and drinks for an entire night out at Cosmo's." It's easily one of the most upscale bars in San Luco, and I grin as Javi and Royer groan—a sure sign of a solid bet.

"And if you lose?"

"If he loses, he covers all *our* food and drinks at Cosmo's." Javi smirks.

Fuck, these guys can put away a lot of food and alcohol, which means a huge tab for me. I don't have trouble getting laid, but my self-selected demographic is already pretty willing—not someone I've legit pissed off. These are high stakes, for sure. I scratch my jaw, considering, then nod. Charm is key, and I have plenty of that. One of the groundskeepers, Lawrence, used to scowl at me every time we crossed paths after I once tossed a sandwich wrapper at a trash can and missed when I was running toward a class I was late for. Then I started giving him a hello when I'd see him and snagging up any extra trash around the bins when I was throwing away something. After six weeks, he started saying hello back. Now we greet each other warmly, and I still pick up lingering trash next to the bins because why not? "I can make it happen." I sound more confident than I am, and I'm definitely gonna have to consider my tactics.

"You know he's in anthro survey with us, right?" Royer says.

"No shit?" There's an avenue that could prove helpful.

"I'm pretty sure, yeah."

"How do you know this?" I rack my brain, but the truth is anthro is one of the gimme courses I don't pay much attention in.

Royer squints. "I have no idea. I think maybe I was checking out the girl he sits next to once and somehow registered him? Mysteries of the universe." He shrugs, then puts a hand over his heart. "I'm pretty sure he's also Darby's best friend. Something like that. Ugh. That woman, I swear." Darby Hawthorne. For the first time, I link the girl Royer has had a weird puppy dog crush on for the last year with Spencer. She was in our bio class sophomore year, and Royer wouldn't shut up about her. They're from the same hometown, and he hung out with her once, if I recall, but I'm pretty sure she shut him down. I thought he'd moved on, but maybe not.

"Did you wake and bake today, man, or what?"

"No." Royer snorts. "My synapses just choose to fire at weird times. Wish they could've helped me out on that calc pop quiz last week, though. Sheesh." He whooshes a hand over his head, and he and Javi, who's in the same class, start bitching about it.

I'm still stuck on sharing a class with Spencer. How have I not noticed him before? Granted, it's a big lecture class that plenty of people take to satisfy their general education requirements, but am I really that unobservant?

Sounds like it's time to remedy that.

ROYER WAS RIGHT. HE AND I FILE IN RIGHT BEFORE THE START OF class, like always, and take our usual spots at the top back left of the lecture hall. I search the crowd carefully until I spy Spencer about three rows back from the front of class on the opposite side, giving me a view of his stern profile as he fiddles with his computer in between chatting with the girl sitting next to him. Why do I find him more attractive every time I look at him? Do I have some sort of fetish for guys who dislike me? Some weird codependency issue that makes me want to win them over? Ugh, that's a deeper thought than I want to get into and definitely too much for 10:00 a.m. I push it aside and try to pay attention to the lecture once the professor begins. Not gonna lie, I often doze off in this class, and our spot at the top is prime for this. I'll pull my ball cap low, slump in my chair, and drift off until Royer thumps me awake or I jump myself awake.

Not today, though.

Today, my attention splits between the professor's Power-Point and Spencer as he diligently taps at his keyboard, taking notes. Judging from what little I know of him, he seems like the serious, rule-following type, which is not my typical style, but now that I've made him my conquest, I need to get to know more about him. So that's what I do for the rest of the class, noticing when his attention drifts, noticing how he keeps his phone face-down on the table, unlike most of the class covertly texting or reading their screens. He's got a little cowlick on the back of his head with one little wayward strand that flutters when the AC kicks on. At one point, the girl he sits with whispers something that makes him smile, and wow, it's something, the tension in his jaw melting and this sexy dimple popping.

When class lets out, I hurry to shove my laptop back in my bag and toss a quick goodbye to a confused Royer as I weave down the aisles, timing it so I drop into step with Spencer and the girl he's walking with as they mill toward the double doors with everyone else.

"Wassup, Nacho?" I ask, cranking my smile up to eleven. It's a proven tactic.

The girl he's with full stops, blinking rapidly at me. "Excuse you?"

Wow. That was abrupt. Has Spencer given her a lowdown on me already? I can't decide if that's a good or bad thing. "I wasn't talking to you. I was—"

She wrinkles her nose. "That's completely inappropriate."

I'm confused now and dart a look at Spencer. His lips are pressed together in a firm line, but I could almost swear amusement dances in his eyes. So he's enjoying this? Fine, I'll roll with it.

"I was talking to Spencer," I explain. "He served me last night, and I ordered nachos, and there was this whole banter-y thing involving nachos. It's just a joke."

"That was banter?" He smirks. Yeah, he's definitely getting some sadistic joy out of this.

"Sounds dumb." The girl wrinkles her nose.

"It was," Spencer assures her. "And I've heard a lot of dumb at Shenanigans."

"Maybe you should try some banter next time that doesn't have insensitive undertones."

Jesus, I can't win. "It wasn't a slur. It was word play." I pin the girl with a look and glance at my watch. "Catch you later, I guess, or not."

"Nacho best effort," Spencer has the gall to call from behind me.

"Nacho problem now," I toss back, then dip. Round one of trying to win Spencer over, much less get him into my bed, is a total fail. Good thing my folks didn't raise no quitter.

I'M RESTLESS ONCE I FINISH MY CLASSES. I CONSIDER THE SLEW OF homework I have to do or disc golf since the weather is ideal. But as the sky takes on the burnished oranges of impending twilight, I find myself heading down to the Luco Landing marina instead.

It's one of my favorite places in San Luco. I grew up in San Diego, but I have lots of childhood memories of sailing off San

Luco's coast with my dad and uncle on my uncle's boats—well, until my parents' firm took off, and then it was often just me and my uncle.

He still has his catamaran here, but that's not where I head today. I bypass all the slips filled with swanky yachts, catamarans, and sailboats on my way toward the charter and fishing slips. Then I plunk down on the end of one of the docks, watching the sky grow pinker and the boats come in one by one.

Jasper's is the third. When he spots me on the dock, he lifts a hand, and I match his wave, hopping up and trotting to the boat slip, ready to catch the line that one of the deckhands, Paolo, tosses to me with a grin.

"Aren't you supposed to be getting that fancy degree?" he teases as I secure the line around a cleat. He says that every time.

"Aren't you supposed to be actually catching fish?" I say that every time, too. But seriously, he has the worst fishing luck. I spent this past summer as a deckhand for Jasper, and Paolo was often relegated to more menial tasks away from the customers so he wouldn't jinx the waters.

"Got a haul today."

"Guess that means you were in the kitchen."

Paolo flips me off with a snort, and I help him secure the rest of the lines.

Jasper appears a minute later, escorting his tired customers off the boat.

"What'd ya get?" I ask.

"Bunch of bluefin mostly, but one of 'em weighed in at 650."

I whistle low. "Need some help?"

"Just can't stay away, can you?"

I shrug as I wait for the last customer to exit and then hop onto the boat. It's true that I have trouble staying away. Working for Jasper was the best job I've ever had. It was a hot, sweaty, smelly job, but the open-air lifestyle made me feel so alive once I learned the routine and got good at working with the other deckhands and customers.

James, another crew member, shows up a moment later, and then we're off, setting the boat back to rights for tomorrow's charters.

I could stay out here all night, and I do linger after we finish, dropping onto one of the seats next to Jasper after James and Paolo head home to their families.

Jasper reaches into his cooler, cracks a beer, and hands it to me. "How's school going?"

"Fine." I shrug and glance around at the boat, so familiar to me now even though I was constantly nervous when I started that I'd fuck something up. "It's school. I'd rather do something like this. I miss it."

Jasper gives me a long look, then shakes his head. "Nah, kid, you're on the right track. This isn't the glamorous life you're used to."

"I know. I was here an entire summer, remember? I loved it."

He chuckles softly. "You can't judge by one summer, you know that, and you're welcome anytime. But you don't need to go throwing away a cushy job for this."

"I didn't say I was," I counter. "Just thinking aloud, I guess." And I'm not even sure it's about the job. I really do like advertising. It's more just trying to imagine myself in an NYC skyscraper that's difficult, cooped up in the winter, and thousands of miles from my home base where I'm comfortable and blue skies are plentiful. Different weather, different people, different lifestyle altogether. I don't know. It's a weird insecurity I have.

Jasper nudges my arm. "I'm glad you came by, though. Got something I've been meaning to ask."

"Hit me." Jasper's more of a rugged do-it-yourself type, so I'm intrigued and a little chuffed that he's asking my dumb ass anything.

"I'm thinking about getting another boat soon—a smaller one—and at the very least updating some of the equipment on this one, which means I'm gonna need a business loan. They've got all sorts a' requirements now they didn't used to have. Wanna see my business plan, maybe even a marketing one, and, well, I'm good at keeping up with my numbers, but..."

"I can absolutely help you with that," I jump in. Business and marketing plans I can do. "I did a business plan for a smaller fishing outfit for my business management 101 final. That's part of what made me want to work with you that summer."

Jasper cracks a crooked grin. "I figured you'd have an idea what to do."

After he ticks off some of his ideas, we lapse into silence, sipping our beer and listening to the peaceful lap of water against the side of the boat, another thing I love about southern California nights. There's almost never a bad time to just hang out by the water, listening to nature. I figure I better soak it in now since, soon enough, I'll be trading it for the noise of city life.

Strolling back through the marina and parking lot a half hour later, I mull the list of information I'll need to get from Jasper, slowing when I spy a familiar car.

Spencer isn't in it, nor is he anywhere nearby when I scan the lot. Since I know he has to be a life sciences major due to living in the LoL house, it's possible he's at one of the hatcheries here. Maybe an evening class? FU has a few different classrooms and research buildings at a marina a short walk from the main campus, but they also have smaller offshoots stationed at marinas like this one in San Luco. Or maybe he's out boating with friends, although, given the tongue-lashing he treated me to recently, it doesn't sound like he has that kind of free time. I wonder where he's from, if he's been out on a boat here or fishing. Would he even like fishing, or would he consider it destroying the earth? I ponder that as I mosey closer to his car and peek in the windows, checking out the interior.

It's neat and well-kept for an older car. No trash in the floorboards or old cups in the cup holders. His apron for Shenanigans is folded neatly on top of two textbooks. Peeking out from underneath the corner of the apron is what looks like a bullet-point list. I can only see one of the items on there, though: fish food. Maybe he has a fish tank. I know a fair deal about fish and had my own tank when I was a kid. There, I've discovered a commonality between us. Now I just have to figure out how to best utilize it.

5

SPENCER

It's not like I'm purposely trying to watch Cory through his window, and it's not like I'm peeking through the blinds constantly. I check maybe once—max twice—a day, and after watching him last time, I told myself I wouldn't spy on any of his shenanigans again, no matter how tempting, because he's an idiot. A hot idiot, but an idiot nonetheless. I remind myself of that as I get back to my room from an evening study group and sneak a peek. It's the first time I've looked today. A lot of times when I check, he's not even there. Makes sense considering the dude seems to have the social life of a Kardashian. On rare occasions, I've spotted him at his desk or scrolling through his phone, probably seeing how many people have liked his most recent Instagram post, because god knows he probably has one.

I pull down the blinds and look real quick, breath catching. He's there, sitting at his desk and shirtless. His back is all hills and valleys and dips, buff shoulders on display that probably a hundred other guys and girls have sunk their teeth into.

He stretches his arms, then laces them at the nape of his neck, rocking back in his chair. Too bad he doesn't tip over. But I'm not that lucky. The muscles of his bicep pop in relief and remind me I really need to start going to the gym again. I've been reminding myself of that for the last eight months and then justify not going because I'm tired and because I get a lot of steps in during my shifts at Shenanigans.

Stop watching, I scold myself at the same moment he relaxes his hands and drifts one down over his pecs, then his nipples. He moves lower still, rubbing his palm over the front of his gym shorts. My jaw clenches in anticipation. Is he gonna... oh fuck. *Fuck*.

Cory hops up, locks his door, then drops back into the chair, typing rapidly on his laptop. My dick is harder than concrete in an instant, and all my willpower to not watch him evaporates faster than water on Texas asphalt as he splays his legs and teases his fingers up and down the front of shorts that start tenting as he watches the screen. Fuck me, I'm about to watch a Cory Ingram solo session. It's intimate and a total violation of his privacy, and... I can't help it. He's right there!

If I don't get off, too, maybe that's better somehow? But dang, the longer I stand there, the more my dick aches, and when he eases his shorts down his thighs and kicks them off, his erection bobbing in the air, I groan aloud and clench a fist to keep from reaching for my own cock.

God, his dick is gorgeous. Not particularly massive in length but thick. He jerks himself dry for a few seconds and then reaches into one of the desk drawers, pulling out some lotion that he squirts on his hand before getting back to work. I can almost hear the wet squish of it as he strokes, and I wonder if he's moaning or if he's the quiet type. Somehow, I don't think so. I can tell by the rise and fall of his chest that his breathing is picking up. He concentrates on his crown, head falling back briefly, eyes closed, teeth sinking into his pouty lower lip, a little grimace forming as his head lolls forward. His eyes open as he concentrates on the screen. *Here it comes*, I think, close to busting my own load, but then he grips his shaft and stops completely.

I can't help a moan as he slowly starts up again, like he's edging himself.

Jesus, I can tell he's trying to restrain the orgasm rising inside him. I know I wouldn't have the wherewithal to do that, but he's so focused; his lips are parted, his eyes are half-lidded, and he's picking up the tempo once more. Pressure gathers in the base of my spine like a storm cloud forming, my hips moving in rhythm with his fist. His strokes become rougher, and his head tips back, the muscles in his neck straining. He's definitely going to come soon. All the signs are there.

I've jerked off to porn before, obviously, but this is so different; this is like spying on a private show, and the fact that it's Cory is somehow all the more erotic. I think about the deep tenor of his voice in class and his stupid nacho jokes. I have to admit he's clever, and the way he was grinning at me, jeez. I need to get ahold of myself before I do something stupid like entertain the idea that he might actually be a decent human being.

He stops again, squeezing the head of his cock between his thumb and forefinger, and I groan at the loss of his strokes when he does.

Then he does something I've never seen anyone do. A jolt of excitement runs through me as he pushes one of his fingers into his mouth, sucking on it like he's sucking a cock, before teasing his crown with it. Never let it be said that Cory doesn't fully enjoy a solo session.

He goes back to work, muscles tensing in his shoulders as he strokes harder and faster. In seconds, he's coming, his pelvis thrusting forward, eyes closed, and teeth gritted. The pleasure etched on his face is as much of a turn-on as the orgasm itself.

Cum slides down his length as he loses it, glistening over his knuckles, but he doesn't let up, just keeps working his shaft until he stops leaking.

My fist moves automatically to keep up with what he's doing. The second I imagine it's my hand on his dick, that it's me milking him dry, I come with a sputtering gasp.

Fuck, why does it have to be Cory in that room? Couldn't it just be some other random frat guy? Would I be as aroused, though, if it were?

A knock on the door pierces through the dangerous thought and has me scrambling to clean up. I manage to get tucked away just as Darby busts in.

"Oh Jesus." She shields her eyes as I cover myself. "Forgot you have a lock?"

"I didn't forget, just got distracted. So go ahead and expect an eyeful the next time you feel like barging in. You realize it's almost midnight?"

"Duly noted." She gives me puppy dog eyes. "I need you to quiz me for Barker's psych exam tomorrow."

"Right now?"

"Yes. That's what good friends do. Plus, I helped you with that god-awful term paper for Medieval Lit last spring."

"Don't remind me." I still have nightmares about Chaucer. "Gimme five and I'm ready."

"Okay, thanks." She pauses in the doorway. "You've probably traumatized Ted."

I snort as we both eye Ted swimming around. "Nah, he's already forgotten. The DIK's stupid late nights are far more offensive."

"You know I'm happy to introduce you to some guys anytime." Darby has been making this offer since the beginning of last year, but I never take her up on it. Maybe senior year. For now, I'm focused on my career path.

With the occasional detour into voyeurism, I guess. "No,

thanks, Darb." I spangle the fingers of my right hand at her. "This baby doesn't require batteries, effort, won't give me an STI, or park in my space." I wince at the unintentional Cory reference, but Darby just laughs and raises her right hand.

"I know. Got my own." She twiddles her fingers, and we do an air high five before cracking up. "By the way, you should wash that thing before we get started."

"C'mon now, I'm not a heathen."

6

SPENCER

I signed up for survey of anthropology because I needed an elective, and considering the intensity of my upper-level eco classes, my advisor suggested this one. Professor Adams is known to be laid-back, the tests are easy, and it's an engaging course for anyone who cares to listen.

I've always been aware that Cory is in the class, but I never paid much mind. He typically sits in the upper back left with some other DIKs, and anytime I've bothered to look before—not often—he's usually asleep. Idiot. But since he caught me off guard with his approach last class, and considering what I saw the other night, my body prickles with awareness as soon as I enter the lecture hall.

I force myself not to look around until I drop into my usual seat, waiting on my friend Gina, and then I attempt what I hope appears to be a casual scan of the other students, brows knitting. The guy he's always with—Royer, I think—is there, but there's no Cory. Probably overslept.

I open my laptop and boot it up, glancing up from my keyboard as the chair scrapes next to me, ready to rag on Gina for cutting it so close.

Cory grins down at me. His tousled hair is too artful to be actual bedhead, and there's a liquid warmth in his dark eyes. I wish he wasn't so dang attractive. I wish the sight of his smile didn't make my cheeks hot and my skin tingle.

"Nope," I say with a shake of my head, and his smile wobbles the tiniest bit. Why the heck does that make me feel bad?

He cocks a brow. "Nope to what?"

I tick my chin toward the chair next to me he's helping himself to. "You can't sit there."

"Of course I can." He chuckles lightly. "What, are we in third grade again? You gonna pull a 'this seat's taken' thing?"

"No, but I am." Gina's thumb is hooked around the strap of her backpack, one hip cocked, a severe look fixed on Cory. God, I love her. "That's my chair." She flicks a wrist. "Shoo."

"Hmmm." Cory peers down at the chair, then quickly examines the table in front. "Don't see your name here."

"So we *are* resorting to third grade tactics," I say, just as Gina waves a hand again.

"Seriously, move your ass before I make a scene."

I don't know Cory at all, but the glint in his eyes suggests he's tempted to see what she'll do. It's his funeral. Gina once chained herself to a tree for twenty-four hours to protest the bulldozing of a historic landmark in downtown San Luco.

When he sits down, Gina promptly sits on top of him, lobbing her backpack onto the table in front of them and cackling when he sputters.

I can't help it—Cory's bewildered expression has me busting up, too.

He raises his hands in surrender. "Fine, fine. Jesus, I'll move."

Gina stands, and Cory shoots me a calculating look as he rises, too. As soon as his ass is out of the seat, Gina puts her foot on it like she's planting a flag.

"Ruthless," Cory mutters. He picks up his backpack only to

skirt around me and move to the empty seat to my left. Beaming at us both, he takes it, undeterred by my scowl.

Then he pulls out his laptop, leaning closer to me. "No one ever sits in this chair."

I clench my molars, the muscles of my jaw fluttering with irritation. "How do you know? Been watching me?" Heat crawls up the back of my neck at the memory of the other night, though it's tinged with shame. Way to be a hypocrite, Spence.

There's a nonchalant flash of his dimple as he punches the power key on his computer. "I notice things." He cuts a sidelong gaze at me again, raking over me from my shoulders upward. Is he...? No fucking way. He's definitely fucking with me. Not that my dick cares. It responds to that slow once-over like it's a caress.

"There's zero reason for you to be sitting next to me. Go back to your DIK brethren." I make the same shooing gesture as Gina.

"I feel like it. There's zero reason for me *not* to be sitting here."

"I can give you one."

He puts a finger behind his ear. "I'm listening."

"I don't like you." Ugh, but I don't hate him, either, and that's an issue.

"I'm sorry to hear that. I like you just fine, although I still feel like yelling at me over a parking space was overkill, and I think you should give me another shot."

"At what, exactly?" I clear my throat. "You know not everyone in the world is gonna like you, right? And that's okay. Part of being a healthy, functioning adult is accepting that fact."

"That sounds like something someone with not very many friends would say." He gives me a dramatically pitying look.

"And your defensiveness sounds like something a person with unhealthy people-pleasing tendencies would say."

A shadow darts through his eyes, and then vanishes just as quickly. "I'm totally good with 98 percent liking me. Sad that the

2 percent misses out, of course, but there's no accounting for personal taste." He inclines his chin toward the front, where Professor Adams is approaching the whiteboard. "Besides, I just wanted a better view today. He's talking about human fossil records. My favorite."

I scoff lightly—I seriously doubt Cory knows what a fossil record is—and he puts a finger to his lips. "Shhhh. Don't distract me, or I'll have to ask you to move."

God, he's infuriating, and the smug little smile that appears on his profile is even worse.

He continues to be distracting as heck through the entirety of class, occasionally leaning over and asking what the professor said or trying to peer at my computer screen as I type.

At one point, he asks if he can borrow a pen.

"You have a laptop," I whisper. "What do you need a pen for?"

"I didn't say I needed one, just asked you if I could borrow one."

"No," I snap a little too loudly. My cheeks flame as, in my periphery, I catch heads turning in my direction. Even the professor stops his lecture, eyeing us.

I shrink down in my seat and focus on the front of the room, trying my hardest to absorb the words coming out of the prof's mouth. But every time Cory shifts, I get a waft of his deodorant or soap or detergent. It's different. Not the usual citrusy-spice scent most guys seem to wear. It's richer without being heavy. Not sandalwood, either. Kinda woodsy, but I can't pinpoint the type, and jeez, am I really going to spend a whole class trying to suss out the composition of Cory's smell between trying to ignore him?

Apparently, the answer is yes because the next thing I know, a general shuffle rises from the hall as people close their laptops, grab their gear, and prep to leave.

"Lunch at the cafe today?" Gina asks, shooting a glare over at Cory as he packs his bag.

"Yeah, I think I can make it."

"K. I gotta jet. Catch up in a bit."

She darts off, and I close my laptop, too. Cory remains, fiddling with something in his pack.

"It's not going to work," I tell him.

He blinks up at me innocently. "What are you talking about?"

"You can't win me over by sheer..." I wave a hand through the air, searching for the right word. "Sheer... pestering. I mean, does that usually work?"

Cory taps his full lower lip, as if pondering. "Not sure. I've never had to try before." His gaze snaps to me, dark and piercing. "So you're assuming I'm trying to win you over." He quirks a brow. "Interesting."

Bateman's principle is interesting. The Gaia hypothesis is interesting. Cory Ingram saying "interesting" somehow just sounds dangerous.

Heat crackles up my spine, forcing me to turn away from his penetrating stare. My body responds way too quickly to this guy. This whole situation is ridiculous. "I think it bothers you that your Mr.-BMOC-friends-with-everyone act doesn't work on me."

"Hmmm. Could be."

I don't dare look over again as I shove my laptop into my backpack, but his response is unexpectedly reflective, as if he's giving it some thought. The whoosh of the zipper on his backpack zings through the air. "Or it could be I just get a kick out of someone who so obviously wants me but is a stubborn ass."

"What?" I balk. "How, during any of our scintillatingly annoying interactions, have I given off the impression that I want you?" Sure, he's attractive, and yes, my dick might respond to him like he's Henry Cavill, and I might have jerked off to him the other night, but that's just a surface-level reaction. There is no way I've outwardly displayed any of that inconvenient and perfectly natural biological response. Inconceivable.

Cory's gaze flickers over me slowly, so slowly it makes me self-conscious. Shit, forget Henry Cavill. Cory's got him beat. I shift on my feet in front of him, but damned if I'm going to back down. I meet his gaze and lift a challenging brow as if to say, *Well?*

"Okay," he replies nonchalantly, then hitches his backpack on his shoulder and steps around me toward the door.

Somehow, the simple response irritates me more than if he'd argued with me.

I don't have time to parse that, though. A quick glance at my watch has me spinning for the door, too, though I let Cory keep his lead before peeling off to the left. I'm in self-preservation mode, and further contact with him isn't a good idea.

***

I stop just outside the dean's office in the Life Sciences building, running a hand over my hair to smooth it back and straightening my shirt before I walk in.

Dean Foster's administrative assistant glances up.

"Spencer Crowe. I just wanted to check in and make sure all of my materials arrived for the environmental policy research internship this spring?"

"Ahh yes, Spencer." I try to gauge her smile and see if it reveals any further information but can discern nothing. Surely the fact that she seems to recognize my name means something? Or is she just being polite? "I've not gone through all of the applications yet to make sure they're complete. I was going to do that tomorrow."

Well, that answers that. The deadline for the applications is tomorrow, though.

"Would it be okay if I wait here while you check mine?" Dang, did that sound overeager? It totally does, but I decide I don't care. I *am* overeager. I want this internship more than anything. It's one of the most prestigious in the entire United States, would be a huge plus on my resume, and also, it's one of the best pipelines for a new college grad into the big think tanks like the GlobalWatch Institute in San Diego, which is my dream job.

"Sure. Give me just a sec." She sorts through a stack of folders on her desk before stopping on one and opening it. She riffles through it, brow furrowing. "Looks good, except one of your professor recommendations is missing. Is there someone else you can ask before tomorrow, or perhaps give the professor a nudge?"

"Which one do you have already?" Panic streaks through me at the near miss. I'm so fucking glad I checked. I have a guess as to which one is missing.

"Connor. So you'll need one more."

"I'm so sorry. Professor Monroe said she'd gladly write me one, but maybe she forgot." I'd loved her class on Fisheries and Aquaculture. My grade had been so high I didn't even have to take the final exam. She's a brilliant scientist but also far more passionate about her work than the accompanying administrative tasks. Or syllabi. She'd go off on tangents constantly during class, which were fascinating to me but annoyed some of the other students endlessly when they weren't relevant to upcoming tests. "I'll go take care of that now."

I know where Professor Monroe will be all afternoon, so after meeting Gina for lunch, I run back to the house and drop off my backpack before taking my car down to the marina on the outskirts of town. One side of Luco Landing is private boats—

mostly catamarans, sailboats, a few swanky yachts. When I first arrived from Texas, I'd walk the perimeter often, just admiring them. I've yet to sail on something that nice, but spring semester of freshman year, I'd gotten my first ever invitation out on a private boat. I'd promptly come down with a stomach bug and couldn't make it. Maybe someday.

The left side of the marina is for commercial fishing boats and charters and is always busy this time of day. Once again, Cory's Jeep is there. I'd noticed it the last time I was here attending one of my evening labs at the fish hatchery. I guess he just has a thing for parking in the wrong place because the private marina has its own lot, and no way that's not where a dude like Cory's going. Unless he decided on a midafternoon fishing trip. I snort at the thought.

My destination is even farther left to an offset dock near a few metal-sided buildings. I breathe in the salty sea air as I walk. Before moving to San Luco, I'd seen the ocean only once in South Texas, and it didn't hold a candle to the serene pacific blue of the waters here.

As I step inside the first building, the trickle of water fills the air from the array of tanks on display. This particular lab is outfitted for more advanced studies and experiments and also has an open area at the front for elementary school classes or summer camps to come through. That's where I find Monroe, giving a tour to a class of what appears to be third or fourth graders.

I wait until she's finished.

"Hey, Spencer." Her smile is warm, and she tips her head. "Wanna come check out these cabezon?"

It's my favorite part of the lab, so I gladly follow her through the doors to the spawning tanks, almost forgetting what I'm here for when I see them.

"Dean Foster's assistant says they didn't get your rec for me."

Monroe's face goes briefly blank, so I tack on, "For the EPR internship? It was due a couple of weeks ago, but it's no problem if I need to ask another professor or if—"

She frowns. "Hold on a moment. I know I filled it out. I wouldn't forget that. I remember doing it." She pulls out her phone and scrolls, then claps a hand to her forehead. "Oh my god, it's still in drafts. I'm so sorry, Spence. I'm sending it right now, and then I'll follow up with a separate email explaining what happened."

Thank goodness. I was nervous she might tell me to get someone else to do it, and since she went through the internship herself, I'm hoping her rec puts me ahead of the other candidates.

We walk through the lab a little longer while she shares some more of the projects underway, and then I tell her I need to head out.

She gives me a hug as we say goodbye, then stops me at the door, tapping her chin. "They haven't set interviews yet?"

"Mrs. Fairley said in the next several weeks."

She nods. "I think you'll get one, and when you go in for it, make sure you're on time and practice some interview questions beforehand." She pauses, canting her head with a smile. "That might be the last occasion I was on time for an appointment. It worked, though." She winks at me.

I absorb her advice, blazoning it on my mind, then thank her and go.

I can't help but look for Cory's Jeep as I leave, but it's gone.

I MAKE THE DRIVE BACK TO CAMPUS, RELIEVED AT KNOWING I'VE gotten everything for the internship squared away now. I worked hard on my application, and I'm feeling optimistic that I have a good shot at the spot.

The mellow vibe lasts until I pull into the LaL lot.

There in my spot is Cory's Jeep.

I growl, gripping the steering wheel. He's definitely fucking with me. And why does that idea elicit the tiniest thrill even as it makes me see red? I glance over at the DIK house lot. Can I steal one of their spots in return? A closer look reveals all of the spots are taken. I wait a few minutes to see if anyone might leave and, when no one does, drive back down the street until I find street parking. Next to the dumpster, of course. I step out of the car and hold my breath to avoid the rank smell. Not even the Shenanigans dumpster can hold a candle to this one. I'm not sure what they're putting in there. Dead bodies?

I stalk back to the house, stopping in front of Cory's car. I should totally just walk over to the DIK house and make him move it. I consider this as I stare at the Jeep's posh leather interior, open to the air, a stupid stuffed yellow smiley face emoji dangling from the rearview mirror. Then my gaze lands on Selena's birdhouses and feeders. She's avid about them, built every single one herself, and then was granted permission by the university to place them outside the LaL house. The lips of the feeders are peppered with birdseed, and as I eye them, a white-crowned sparrow swoops down, nibbles at the seed, and promptly decorates the ground below with droppings. A large portion of the ground below the feeders is dotted with bird poop, in fact.

I shouldn't. I *really* shouldn't.

But that same little thrill that shot through me earlier takes a mental exit onto a more devious route.

Inspired, I grin as I head inside the house and go straight for the pantry, where I dig around until I find the birdseed.

Back outside, I scoop out handfuls of the stuff and, with a

quick peek around to make sure no one's nearby, scatter it all over Cory's car. The seats, the floorboards, the footwells, even the hood. At best, Cory returns to a car that looks like an avian Rorschach, but at the very least, the birdseed will be a pain in the ass to get out.

I briefly consider the ethics of this venture. But screw it. Cory's messing with me? I'll mess with him back.

I return to the house, superbly smug, and head to my room to study, but the desire to sneak a peek at Cory's car keeps distracting me. I don't have a view from my window, though. I wish I'd had a camera to set up, just to see his reaction.

Nacho that, Cory Ingram.

I drop my pencil and jump up. Shit. Shit! Literal shit. What if the birds peck the paint off Cory's car in addition to shitting all over it? Is car paint susceptible to bird beaks and repeated pecking? Maybe Selena would know. Cleaning up a bunch of bird poop is one thing, but needing a whole new paint job? Fuck. Why didn't that occur to me before? Yes, technically he parked in my space, and he did it to antagonize me, but still, that doesn't necessarily deserve a bunch of birds ruining his paint job permanently.

Visions of a bunch of DIKs storming into the LaL house, pitchforks blazing, have me rushing to the door. I need to go make sure that prolific pecking doesn't occur.

I fling open the door to my room and nearly slam into a mountain of delightfully scented, muscular, T-shirt-encased chest.

Cory. Crap.

"Oof." I jump back instinctively and knock my funny bone against the doorjamb. "Ahhh, god. Fuck. It's never funny. Never ever funny."

"Kinda funny to me, to be honest, and also, you deserve it."

I search Cory's face, attempting to discern how pissed off he is on a scale of mildly irritated to DIK storming en masse. His scowl maybe puts him in the five range, which is possibly survivable.

He levels that sharp brown gaze on me. "There's bird shit all over my car, Spencer."

With relief, I note he didn't say anything about his paint job. Dare I hope?

I rub my elbow and clear my throat, trying to compose myself. "Sparrows are native to this area. Guess your Jeep attracted them."

Denial, the best defense.

"Birds are primarily attracted to red, though some seed-eating types prefer blue or silver. Army green, not so much. Thanks, G'ma." Cory kisses two fingers and lifts them to the sky as I stand there dumbstruck. Cory knows about birds? Interesting. "Where'd you get the birdseed? Think you're pretty clever, huh?"

"I... yeah. I mean, no. I'm not clever, and I don't know what you're talking about. Birdseed? What?" I make a face that I hope portrays extreme but natural bewilderment.

"Jesus, you're a bad liar." Cory pushes past me into my room.

"Come right in, I guess. I mean, you help yourself to everything else of mine." I rub at the electric tingle on my bicep where he brushed against me.

"Everything?" Cory shoots a look over his shoulder that heats my groin more than it should, especially given my current predicament. I know he doesn't mean it that way, but still. I brush it aside, along with the accompanying thrill that sneaks up my spine over Cory being in my room. Dang testosterone.

"You want my covers? Some of my clothes? Maybe my desk?"

Cory doesn't answer immediately. He's stopped in front of my fish tank and bends lower, squinting at Ted. "A crowntail betta. Pretty. What'd you name him? Her?"

"Ted," I answer automatically, then tack on with alarm, "You can't have him."

"Is he the only one?"

"I'm going to add some pygmy cories next week and then—" Wait. What the fuck am I doing actually engaging with him on a conversational level?

"Cories would be good. Cool name, too." He chuckles in amusement at himself. "Where'd the birdseed come from? And I assume you're going to clean up the crap spackling my car now before it ruins my paint job, yeah?"

"Yeah. I mean, no. I mean, have no idea what you're talking about." I lace my fingers in front of me primly. It's the sort of picture of innocence that seems to work in movies.

"God, it's getting worse. Look, if you're going to lie, it's helpful to look someone straight in the eye, and what are you doing with your hands? You look like an antique person posing for a portrait."

Antique person. Nope, not even going to touch that.

"Sorry, I'm not adept at lying like a pro. It's not something I'm in the habit of doing." Much.

"At least you admit you're lying now."

"Wait, what? No, I didn't. I..." Totally did.

Cory's gaze flickers back to my tank. "You could do some guppies, too, if you wanted more color since the cories are kinda bland."

"I thought about that. Maybe after I see how Ted handles the cories." Great, now I'm taking tank advice from a frat guy.

Cory nods as if satisfied, spins around, and starts toward the door again, glancing down at his watch. "I'll be back from class in an hour and a half. I assume you'll have my car cleaned up by then."

"And I assume if I were to go down and clean it, which is not an admission of guilt, by the way, that it will no longer be in my parking spot."

"Oh no, it'll still be there." Cory sweeps past me. "You should name one of your cories after me. And if you ever want any lessons on lying with a straight face, just lemme know."

"Asshole," I mutter.

"It's Cory, actually, but I've answered to Asshole before. Depends on the tone of voice." He clucks his tongue with a little chuckle and thunders down the stairs, easy as you please.

I stare into the empty hallway after him, then turn around and watch Ted swimming in his tank. Cory knows about fish. And birds. That is... surprising. Maybe intriguing, too, but before the thought can sink its hooks too deep, I steel my jaw and head downstairs. He's still an infuriating idiot, after all.

Five pairs of eyes glom onto me as I walk into the living room.

"What?"

"What? Really?" Chance's eyes widen. "That was Cory Ingram. In our house. Looking for you. Do you know him? Are you friends? God, he's hot."

"Psht. No. I don't know him, he just keeps parking in my fucking spot."

"I'd let him park in my spot."

"Please." Selena sniffs. "Cory can lay anyone he wants, and I doubt it would be anyone from this house."

"Why not? It's not like he's that discriminating," I scoff right back.

"He looks like a model." Chance gestures around. "We do not. He wouldn't give a single one of us the time of day. We look like the C team for PacSun."

Darby cracks up. "No, we're the people who stand in for the shot composition while the models get ready."

"Pfft. Not even that."

Indignation pricks at my skin. For one, I think I'm pretty cute, relatively speaking. Yeah, okay, maybe all together we sort of resemble the cast of *Freaks and Geeks*, but we are all definitely fuckable. Geek chic is a thing. "Cory's a total tool."

"Really? He was pretty nice when he came in. Introduced himself and everything, as if we needed an introduction," Chance says.

"He bought our entire study group dinner once," Walt chimes in, poking his head out of the kitchen.

"It's just a front. He's a seething asshole underneath, trust me." Why am I getting so many skeptical stares? "He is," I insist.

"So what did he want with you, then?"

"I... well, he parked in my space again, so I poured a bunch of Selena's birdseed all over his Jeep." I wince with the admission.

Darby cackles, but Selena looks pissed.

"I'll expect you to compensate me for the birdseed, then. And sorry, in my opinion, that was a dick move. You could have just asked him to move the car."

I throw up my hands. They won't get it.

Lifting my chin haughtily, I stalk to the kitchen, grab a roll of paper towels to go clean off Cory's stupid Jeep, and head outside.

I would laugh at the sight if I wasn't the one about to have to deal with this mess because Cory's car is absolutely spattered with bird shit. This will take at least an hour. But probably longer.

Fuck my life.

7

CORY

Not gonna lie, anthro class with Spencer has become one of the highlights of my week.

When I slide into the seat on his left on Thursday, his exasperated eye-roll makes me grin. I expect he'll spend the rest of class trying to ignore me, as usual.

But this time, there's an interesting development. After a huff of annoyance, Spencer reaches into his backpack and tosses me a pen. "Here."

A pen offering? Oh my. This could be a positive sign. Maybe he's feeling crappy for the Shitpocalypse he unleashed on my Jeep the other day. "What's this for?"

"Since I've given you a pen, you can't ask me for one."

Ah. I nudge the pen back in his direction. "I don't need one, but thanks."

"Yes, but you're going to ask for one regardless, just to annoy me. Now you can't ask because I've already given you the thing you're going to ask for. And since I'm generous, you can keep it." His smirk says he's pleased with himself for this preemptive strike.

I scratch my jaw and nod, hooking the pen to the collar of my tee. "Alright, fair."

He eyes me dubiously, but I play angelic, facing forward and retrieving my laptop so I can take notes.

Then, once the professor walks into class and gets started, I lean over, inhaling the clean scent of him—he always smells damn good—and whisper, "Do you have a pencil I can borrow?"

Spencer's nostrils flare with irritation, and he squeezes his eyes shut briefly before exhaling a slow breath and angling slightly toward me, speaking softly. "No one uses pencils anymore. You don't need a pencil, just like you don't need a pen. And don't tell me you just want one because guess what? I want things that I don't get, too. Like more than four hours of sleep on a regular basis. Or a catamaran. An endless supply of Orange Sours. Or how about just getting through this class one time without you asking me for something. I could go on."

"Gentlemen, is there a problem?" the prof asks, and we both quickly answer, "No," in unison.

Ten minutes later, while the professor is setting up his next PowerPoint, I turn to Spencer again. "Did you add any cories to your tank yet?"

At first, he seems like he's not going to answer, and then he presses his lips together and exhales. "Maybe."

"Sweet, did Ted adjust okay?"

"He did, but..." Spencer stops, shaking his head. "Quit doing that."

"What, trying to have a conversation with you?"

"Yeah, that."

"The sheer audacity, me trying to converse with my tablemate, right?" In my defense, Spencer could shut me down easily if he wanted, but that's not the vibe he puts out at all, so I press on. "I have to know... did you name any of the cories after me?"

"No." He does that thing where he presses his lips together

again. "One Cory is enough in this world, trust me."

"I'm glad you think I'm enough for you. I mean, I've never had any complaints or anything, but you never know."

Next to Spencer, Gina is laughing. He elbows her.

"See, I've even won Gina over."

She leans around Spencer. "You've not won me over. You're just such a pest that I can't help but be entertained."

Ouch. I grin winsomely anyway. "I'll accept that."

"Is there anything you don't accept?" Spencer narrows his eyes at me, and I know he means that as a dig at my reputation, probably, but I'm not gonna give it to him, no matter how much I'm tempted to point out that foot traffic in my bedroom has been virtually nonexistent lately. What's even stranger is that I haven't given it much thought. I've been a little preoccupied.

"There are plenty of things I don't accept. I don't accept ranch dressing as anything less than a universal condiment like ketchup. I don't accept that the Tigers won the Super Bowl last year. The Denver Rush totally deserved that one—fight me. And I don't accept that you don't find me at least mildly entertaining."

"Gentlemen." Professor Adams gives us a stern stare. Oops. "Unless you're fervently discussing the evolution of Neanderthals, I suggest you wrap it up."

Under his breath, Spencer murmurs, "You *are* a Neanderthal."

"Ooga booga," I grunt in reply and face forward.

Once class lets out, I linger, waiting for Royer.

"Things are going swimmingly, I see." He cracks up, and I thwap him.

"Long game. I swear he's coming around."

"Uh-huh. Nice pen, by the way."

I pull the collar of my shirt out, examining the logo on the pen I'd failed to pay any attention to earlier. It reads "Clinic for

Erectile Dysfunction" with a lovely slogan beneath in italics. "We get your meat back on its feet."

Well. There's a business that could definitely use some branding help. But that also reminds me I need to get started on Jasper's business plan for his loan.

BACK AT THE DIK HOUSE, I PEEL OFF MY SHIRT AND GROAN AS cool air from the vent above hits my sweaty skin, skittering goose bumps across my pecs and abs, along with a delicious little tingle. I'm hornier than usual today. I guess bantering back and forth with Spencer got me all worked up.

I could have someone here and ready to go in a half hour. What I don't get is why I haven't done that. Instead, I close my eyes, an image of Spencer on his knees in front of me surfacing, his face upturned, his hand on my cock. I groan again, my dick hardening as I imagine the opposite. Me lowering to my knees in front of him, the tremor in his thighs as I take him into the back of my throat and suck him relentlessly until he falls apart, all those scowls and irritated huffs he aims in my direction during class reduced to whimpers and the clutch of his fingers in my hair. Fuck yeah, it would be highly satisfying to make Spencer Crowe come so hard he forgets his own name. Or, even better, yells mine.

My eyes flutter open as I shove a hand in my shorts and give my erection a couple of strokes. My hand hasn't seen this much action in years, and I'm thinking, again, about remedying that with another actual human when something catches my eye. It's not movement, exactly, because when I turn fully and look out the window, all I see across from me are the shabby closed blinds on another window of the LoL house.

But I felt that undeniable sense of presence. Electricity tightens my balls and races up my spine as I watch. Nothing moves, but I know without a doubt I was being watched. I suppose most people would find that intrusive, to say the least. Possibly even offensive or stalkerish, but I've always kind of had a thing for exhibitionism. Not enough to risk being arrested for public indecency or anything—aside from the one streaking incident. But someone watching me touch myself? Fuck yeah, I'm into it.

It's not until a moment later that I slow my hand as it shuttles up and down my cock and then go still as I narrow my eyes at the blinds across the way. There are spots where the slats have gone crooked or are drooping, a few chunks missing altogether. I can't see anything through them, but someone could easily peek out and see enough of me. And something about the way they hang is familiar...

My brain connects the dots in a rush. My visit to the LoL house the other day, Spencer's room on the second floor, the large double windows covered by blinds.

The one facing mine.

Well, well, what do we have here?

I turn away to hide the beginnings of a smile, and there comes that prickling awareness again. I'm pretty sure Spencer Crowe, that sneaky sneak, is watching me.

And I don't hate it one bit.

My dick throbs as I push down my boxers, then kick them off.

Fuck it, if he's gonna watch, I'm going to give him a show he won't forget.

I go to my closet, rummaging through the upper shelf until my fingers brush over soft, cool silicone. It was a drunken internet purchase just for shits and giggles, and I haven't used it in an age because, usually, there's a real ass for me to push into.

But as I pull the thing down and set it up on the edge of the bed, it gets me turned on. Correction, the idea of Spencer watching me fuck a silicone ass gets me turned on. Way more than if it were just me alone.

I'm dripping precum by the time I squirt some lube onto the tight little hole and push it inside. Spencer's so damn uptight, I bet his ass is the same. I'd relish pushing my fingers inside him, forcing him to loosen up for me.

Shit, I can't delay any longer.

I lube up my dick, wipe the excess off onto my thigh, and then pin the silicone ass in place with one hand, the other guiding my crown into the puckered pink flesh. I'd forgotten how realistic it could feel, even lacking human body temperature.

The smooth passage grips my cock perfectly, and I brace my hand on the mattress, still holding the ass in place with the other as I slowly start to fuck into it. My eyes roll back in my head with pleasure flooding through me, imagining it's Spencer's hip I'm gripping. Imagining that my staggered breaths are matched by his, imagining the moans he'd let out as I move faster. And faster. Plunging deep inside him, then short and shallow, angling for his prostate, making him cry out.

Less than five minutes later, I'm the one crying out as my orgasm builds to a dizzying crescendo and crashes over me. As I erupt, I pull out until just the tip of my cock is inside and jerk my shaft, milking the orgasm for all it's worth. Cum oozes out of the pinched silicone hole, leaking down the sides of the asscheeks. When the last shudder of orgasm ebbs, I drop onto my knees, both hands gripping the silky soft flesh of the toy and squeezing as I lean forward, flicking my tongue over the hole I've just fucked into bliss, tasting myself. Get a load of that, Spencer Crowe. Literally.

I'm kinky that way. Sue me.

8

SPENCER

Cory Ingram is trying to kill me, and he's fully aware of it. Sitting next to me in class every day smelling good, looking good, and popping that stupid dimple every time he teases me? That's one hundred percent on purpose.

But it's the window shenanigans that are ultimately driving me crazy, and that's my fault. I left teeth marks in my own hand trying not to cry out as I came watching him fuck a silicone ass. How the hell was he able to make fucking a lump of silicone so damn hot? Pure devilry.

And it's got to stop.

The sitting next to me, the teasing banter, me watching him. All of it.

So that's what I resolve to do a few days later when I realize I almost forgot to feed Ted and the cories because I got distracted checking the window. Again.

Enough is enough.

I'm going to march over to the DIK house, where I know he's upstairs working because I saw him through said window, and I'll call a truce.

And then I'll never watch him again.

For real.

Once I get to the frat house, I have no idea whether to go in one of the back doors or the front. I default to the back and knock. No answer.

When I twist the handle, the door opens, so I step inside, calling out a hello.

I hear movement from one of the rooms. Then a rumple-haired guy appears in a doorway, munching on a banana. I don't recognize him, but he gives me an upnod between bites. He's a smacker. Ew.

"Hey. I'm here to see Cory."

He looks me over, a faint smile tinging his lips. "Room 24."

"Thanks," I mutter, already heading toward the set of stairs I spotted at one end of the hall.

I stop just outside of Cory's door and glance down at myself, straightening my shirt and smoothing back my hair. Nerves skitter through me before I roll my shoulders and square them. I can do this. Then I knock on the door.

"S'open."

Stepping inside, I'm immediately flustered by the scent I've been trying to peg. "Wow... it's..." Totally beside the point. Back on track, Spence.

Cory pushes back in his desk chair and eyes me, arching a brow. "Hello."

"Hey, I..." Am totally losing my train of thought.

"Came to tell me you've coated my car in syrup? Sprayed it with shaving cream? Doused it with a hose?"

"No, but the syrup idea isn't bad." I ease the door closed behind me. "I came to, um... god, what is that scent?"

"Huh?"

"That smell—it's like mossy and smoky but somehow light and fresh and... I don't even know what else." Probably a good thing I'm an ecology major and not a copywriter.

Cory runs a hand through the damp ends of his hair. "It's bodywash and a cologne from TGS, this company whose account my parents' firm holds. Really cool brand. All organic, none of the bad shit. Hence TGS, The Good Shit. The problem with those sometimes is the fragrance doesn't hold, but they've figured it out somehow." The unexpectedly impassioned response throws me. I had no idea Cory got excited about anything other than partying and getting laid. I catch the deodorant stick he tosses me and open the cap for a sniff. Heavenly. "I got a bunch of free product because I sat in on one of their strategizing meetings once to try to help tap into the younger demographic. That's also why their Instagram is so badass." He buffs his nails on the shoulder of his tee. "Anyway, you were saying you came to... what?"

Right. Back to the task. I set the deodorant down on his dresser and falter again as I realize how flimsy my game plan is. As in, there isn't much of a game plan at all. "I came to—" Jeez, this is the second time I've been alone with Cory, and it's even more overpowering in a way that makes me tingly and off-kilter.

"Apologize for being an absolute dick? Please carry on."

"Hold on a minute. I wasn't an absolute dick."

Cory seesaws his hand. "Carpet bombing a dude's car in birdseed is pretty absolute."

"So is repeatedly parking in someone else's parking space just because you can and then annoying them in class," I counter.

"Much less dickish." Cory pushes out of his chair and swipes a T-shirt from the floor, tossing it on his bed.

"Who determines the scale of dickishness?" I say, then sigh. "Fine, yes. I apologize for the dick move with the birdseed. Can we come to some kind of truce? You don't park in my space, and you tell your bros not to park in my space. I won't mess with your car. And you also stop sitting next to me in anthropology."

Cory grins. "But I like sitting next to you in class."

"No you don't." I know he's lying, even if him saying that makes my stomach swoop. "You just do it to annoy me."

"I fall asleep less when I'm sitting there."

"Then sit somewhere else in the front."

"Tell you what." Cory drops onto the end of his bed, steepling his fingers, his dark eyes calculating. "The way I see it, you still kinda owe me." He lifts a finger when I start to protest. "You do. So you can do me one simple favor in return, and then, sure, truce. Easy peasy."

I wait impatiently as his smile grows and finally prompt him to continue with an arch of my brow. "Well?"

"You go out with me and—"

"No." Pretty sure the single-syllable word breaks speed records rushing from my tongue. "That's the worst idea I've ever heard." More time with him is the exact opposite of what I need.

Cory continues on unperturbed. "Yes, and you get your friend Darby on board. Me, you, Royer, and Darby all hang out."

Bewilderment shakes loose my curiosity before I can say no again. "Darby? Why the hell would Darby hang out with Royer?"

"She wouldn't." Cory finger guns me. "That's where you come in. Royer really digs her, and he tells me you're Darby's best friend. Dude, this is an easy task. You don't have to make some big production out of it. It's just four people hanging out."

"Two of whom don't want to be 'hanging out.'" I roll my eyes. "This is stupid. Let's just call a truce and be done with it."

Cory shakes his head slowly. "Nope. This is the deal. Otherwise, it's open season on your space, and I send you the bill for when I had to have the Jeep detailed after your little birdseed experiment."

"I cleaned it up!"

"You and I both know it had to be detailed after that."

I groan because I can't deny it. I'd done the best I could, but there had been spots I couldn't get to with just rags, soapy water, and a vacuum. "So you're blackmailing me?"

Cory twists his mouth to one side. "I'd consider it more like... calling in a favor."

Spending more time with him sounds like a terrible idea, and I'm not confident I can get Darby to agree to this, but if it means he'll leave me alone afterward, I'll do my best. "Fine. One double date, which I can guarantee you isn't going to do either of you any favors, and then we're done."

"One double date and we're done. Agreed."

But I don't believe the mischievous twinkle in his eyes. At all.

"Absofuckinglutely not!" Darby exclaims.

A library aide shushes her loudly, and Darby leans closer to me at the table where we've parked to study together, hissing. "I can't even believe you'd consider going out with Cory. You hate that dude."

Hate is a strong word. Dislike might be better. Or maybe something slightly lesser than dislike. Wait, what am I thinking? Dislike is the perfect word.

"I sort of owe him." In my own mind, the birdseed incident isn't enough to accept what suspiciously sounds like a double date, but the tiny twinge of guilt over watching Cory through his window pushed me over the edge. The guy has unwittingly been giving me private shows and some of the most powerful orgasms I can remember in months. I've given it more consideration and decided if he wants some bullshit hangout session to continue his stupid ploy to bring me into his fan club and give his buddy

Royer a shot with Darby that's gonna blow up in his face? Well, that doesn't sound like such a bad trade.

And then we'll be through with each other once and for all.

Darby groans as I finish my explanation. "Nope, not doing it. I don't like Royer. Never have."

"What do you have against him, exactly? I didn't even know you knew him that well."

She sighs. "I grew up with him. We went to middle and high school together. He was a popular kid, obviously. And I was... me."

"Fierce, intelligent, and gorgeous, you mean?" I say, and she flashes me a brief smile as she pats my arm.

"Silly flatterer. In middle school, I had glasses, braces, the whole nine. Believe me when I say the transformation from geek to chic geek was a long road." She nudges her glasses with a knuckle. She has a ton of pairs, but the cat-eye frames she's wearing today are my favorites. "In eighth grade, there was a school dance. My mom made me go. Me and my fellow loser brigade hung out on the bleachers in the gym the whole time, and then out of the blue, Will Royer came over and asked me to dance. I couldn't believe it. I thought he was cute. Everyone did. I thought I might pee my pants I was so beside myself."

Now I'm leaning in with interest. I can't believe she's never told me this before. "And what, he just left you there on the dance floor and embarrassed you like some teen rom-com?"

She frowns. "No. We actually did dance to the song. He was nice enough. Asked me about my dress and told me about his dog. Then that was it. No more dances. The next day, I found out it had been a dare. His stupid friends had dared him to dance with the biggest nerd in the school, and he determined that was me. So fuck him."

Now it's my turn to frown, and I can't believe I'm about to say this, but... "That was eighth grade, Darby. Everyone does dumb shit in eighth grade."

"Don't care." She shrugs, and I can tell she's trying to come off as nonchalant, but something about her expression makes me skeptical.

I narrow my eyes at her. "You still like him."

"I do not!" When the library aide shushes her again, she shoots him a glare but lowers her voice. "He's a DIK. And a dick. Both of those aspects are nonstarters for me." I give her puppy dog eyes, and she shakes her head. "Don't try to lay a guilt trip on me."

"I helped you prep for psych the other day. And when you were trying to get with that blond bio major last year, I suffered through a double date with Rich." Ugh. That guy had had the worst breath I'd ever experienced in my life. And he was a loud-talker, too. I tack on my most baleful look for added emphasis. "It's one time, and then we never have to deal with them again. Please? I need this."

She stares at me for a long time before exhaling gustily. "If I do this, you should feel guilty for guilt-tripping me, and you should also know that I'm only doing it for the privilege of putting Will Royer in his place. If you're smart, you'll do the same. Those guys are tools. They have some dumb scoreboard tracking how many people they sleep with," she says, repeating campus legend. I have no idea if it's true or not, though the amount Cory gets around, I wouldn't doubt it. He goes after sex like it's his job, even if he hasn't brought anyone home in the last couple of weeks. I wonder what's up with that but squash the thought anyway. None of my business.

And, with any luck, that will stand permanently after this stupid double date.

9

SPENCER

"Disc golf?" Darby stares down at the plain white disc Royer's holding out to her and then folds her arms over her chest. "I literally couldn't think of a worse way to spend an afternoon."

"What's wrong with disc golf? It's fun, it's outdoors, it's a beautiful day..." Dejection leaks into Royer's voice.

The way he watched her as we approached the course earlier makes me think he really does have a thing for her. Color me shocked. Not because Darby isn't cool or pretty, but because Royer is the archetypal frat guy, right down to his patterned board shorts and the hard part in his glossy blond hair. He looks like a Ken Doll waiting on his Barbie.

Next to me, Cory is smirking. At me, at the situation, all of it, probably.

Darby gestures around the grassy, treed area. "Here I was thinking picnic, or..."

"Do you like picnics?" Royer's eyes light with hope.

"Not particularly. But I like them better than disc golf."

"Damn, tough customer," Cory mutters under his breath.

"I've never even thrown a Frisbee."

"What?" Cory and Royer exclaim in such horrified unison that I almost bust out with a laugh. Frat dudes, I swear.

"I've been busy doing important things like, oh, coursework, getting a degree."

They continue back and forth, and I jump when Cory nudges me. "Have you thrown a Frisbee before?"

"Sure, but never like this. I hope you both have a lot of patience because this is gonna be a long game."

Cory's grin is undeterred. "We have plenty, don't you worry, Spence."

"Stop calling me that. Friends call me that."

"Spence…er. What about just 'errrrrr'? Like the sound you make anytime you look in my direction?" He claws the air to drive the point home.

Once again, he's grinning, and fuck, I can't turn away fast enough before a smile starts to form. He's annoying, not cute, I remind myself. Okay, he's cute. And hot. But the annoyance factor carries more weight than the cute and hot. Or should. "Just Spencer works great, thanks."

Darby and I do our best to look bored as the pair of idiot DIKs explain the rules of the game and the different Frisbees… er, discs, and what they're for. But both Darby and I have competitive streaks, and once the game is underway, we get into it in spite of ourselves.

It's pretty fun, and we all rib each other relentlessly. Darby picks up the game quickly for not having ever tossed a Frisbee before, and I'm not horrible, either. Royer and Cory are, of course, impressively skilled at a sport I didn't know existed, much less required finesse.

But jeez, watching Cory is killing me inside with every tee off. He's wearing a T-shirt and shorts, nothing special about that. But his body is so damn fit, and every time he flings the Frisbee, a variety of muscles on his upper arm pops just like they did the other day when he was fucking the silicone ass.

At least I can blame the flush in my cheeks on the heat.

At the last hole, Cory stands on the tee box, judging his distance with deliberate focus, jaw tense and locked, before his arm slices through the air. The disc soars with impressive speed before landing about twenty-five yards from the goal. Hole. Whatever the heck it's called. The rest of us take our turns, me last.

I judge my distance, tongue pinned to the corner of my mouth, eyes narrowed. I think I've got this. Darby hoots an encouragement. Royer, too, and just as I rear back to make my throw, Cory joins in with a clap that totally jolts me.

The disc goes sailing, and at first, I think I've managed to salvage it anyway, but then it cuts sharply left and vanishes within a stand of trees.

"Goddammit," I mutter and then whirl on Cory. "You did that on purpose!"

He puts his hands up immediately. "I didn't, I swear." He even sounds like he means it, but I'm not sure whether to believe his tone. Or the sparkle of mirth in his eyes.

I flip him off as I head toward the copse of trees and shrubs. The vegetation is short and scrubby, dotted with sumac. You'd think a white disc would be easy to find in this kind of setting, but it's not.

I end up on my hands and knees, picking through the fronds while grumbling.

"Looking for this?"

A sumac frond lances my cheek as I shoot upright. I rub it irritably as Cory waves the disc in the air.

"I've searched this whole area. Where the hell was it?"

He points off to the left. Okay, fair. I hadn't gotten to that spot yet.

"Great. Thanks." I reach out to snatch it from his hand, but Cory won't let go. In fact, he gives it a tug, upsetting my balance so that I'm forced to catch myself before I fall into him. My palms land squarely on his chest.

Smooth, firm pecs and... *fuck.* I quickly regain my balance and drop my hands. Touching him is not a good idea.

"Not so fast. Spence. Er."

"They're waiting on us."

"Nope, pretty sure Royer's making some inroads with Darby. Let's give them a minute."

"Fine," I say, though I have my doubts about whether Royer's and Darby's idea of inroads intersect.

Silence drops between us, thicker than the humidity, and I become painfully aware of Cory's proximity, his usual delicious smell made stronger by the heat. Why the heck can't he stink of BO or something?

Shielding my eyes, I gaze beyond the copse in search of Darby and Royer but can't find them. When I turn my head again, Cory's eyes are on me, roaming freely. Torso, thighs, face. The sharp quip I mean to make dies on my tongue as his gaze moves slowly up my chest, my neck, to my mouth, and then my eyes, where they lock. He's not even trying to be subtle. Is it suddenly ten degrees hotter? Just me? Cory has a powerful stare, I'll give him that.

I can't help it—I check out his mouth, even though I know damn well what it looks like. But not from this close, where I'm acutely aware of its pink hue, the breadth of his lower lip, and the plump Cupid's bow at the top that would probably feel amazing to suck on.

"See something you like?" His voice is low and sultry. Oh yes, he knows exactly what he's doing. How many other women and men has he said it to before? How many of them have denied him? Even with that awareness, I still splutter when he leans closer. "Is it my mouth? All you have to do is ask. Told you before, I'm generous."

God, he's so close that I can feel the warmth of his breath against my lips, smell a tinge of shaving cream.

I step back. "You're arrogant is what you are. Come on."

His chuckle follows me as I stride back out onto the rolling green of the disc golf course. Darby and Royer are walking toward us. Darby looks... not exactly displeased, but judging by Royer's expression, whatever solo time they had clearly didn't go as he'd hoped.

Either way, I figure it's a good time to wrap this up. "I guess we're about done here, yeah?"

"We should go grab some food and drinks first," Royer blurts. I've kinda gotta admire his persistence, and, wow, Darby surprisingly doesn't shoot him down immediately. But she hedges with a little hum before shooting a questioning glance at me.

"I dunno..."

"Nah, that sounds like a great idea," Cory says, aiming a pointed you-still-owe-me look in my direction.

So off to Shenanigans we go, the vision of Cory's mouth close to mine like the afterimage of a lightning strike burned permanently into the back of my mind.

Cory and Royer seem to know everyone in the bar and spend a few minutes doing the usual fratboy social mating calls, fist-bumping, greeting people. Leading Darby to a free table, I upnod coworkers and the single non-employee I vaguely know playing open mic night, Chris, but he's fixated on a broody-looking guy standing alone anyway.

Once we're seated and Royer and Cory join us, we order our food, nursing a pitcher of beer while Darby sips an extra-dirty martini. It quickly becomes obvious the DIKs are struggling for conversation topics, and Darby and I are no help. Sorry, boys.

I nudge her leg under the table, eliciting a tiny smile. I know she's thinking the same thing: let them work.

Royer fiddles with his napkin. "So I'm the social chair, and I'm working on our fall fundraiser. You might have heard of it before. Or been to it?" His eyes are hopeful as he looks at Darby. I've heard of it. It's one of the biggest events around, usually a rager, and draws a huge Greek crowd. It's not exactly our scene, though. Or the scene of anyone else we know.

She squints at him and cocks her head. "You mean those parties you throw where you sell a couple of raffle tickets so you can pat yourselves on the back for 'serving your community' while getting hammered?"

Royer exhales a measured breath and, once again, I have to commend his fortitude. "We raised 15k last year for St. Jude's. It's not just lip service. And for this year's charity, I lobbied hard for our fundraiser to benefit cystic fibrosis." His voice goes softer. "I don't know if you remember, but my older brother has it."

I glance over at Darby, who looks properly cowed. At least now I'm not the biggest jerk in the room.

"I'd forgotten that, I'm sorry. That sounds like a great charity," she amends, which is probably as gracious as I've ever seen her be.

I'll give it to Royer. He doesn't seem to be one to hold a grudge or kick a person when they're down. He plants his chin on his palm and fiddles with a straw. "I was trying to think of a cool theme. Something new. Something that might be appealing for the usual attendees but also maybe other folks who aren't into…"

"A Barbie and Ken theme?" Darby supplies, sipping daintily

at her martini, a wicked glint returning to her eyes that has me coughing to cover a laugh.

"Yeah, not that." Royer snap points at her. "Either of you have any ideas?"

Boy, this dude really is desperate if he's asking me and Darby for ideas.

"Matches made in hell. The nine circles of hell. Everyone dresses according to their circle. *Paradise Lost* theme. Ohhhhh, or a *Scarlet Letter* theme," she chirps, clearly enjoying herself.

"Those seem a little, ummmm.... dark, maybe?" Royer ventures diplomatically. "But you might be onto something with the whole costume bit."

"Please don't do famous couples throughout time." She fake gags.

"What about cosplay?" I suggest. Cory seems confused, so I continue. "Pick any movie, book, or TV series, and so on, and dress up as a favorite character. Your average frat partygoer will love the chance to dress up. Your non-frat types might be drawn in by the cosplay itself. You could make the event like a con—a convention—" I explain. "That's where you'll see a lot of cosplay happening, but there's not another major one in our area until after the new year, so there'd probably be plenty of interest."

"Damn." Cory nods enthusiastically, then eyes me consideringly. "You might be onto something here. So do you cosplay?"

"He makes a killer Spider-Man."

"That's my go-to." I swallow a sip of beer. "But I also did Willy Wonka once, and that was pretty cool."

"Oh yeah," Darby cackles. "That was a great one, too."

"What do you think?" Royer asks, addressing Darby. "Would you come to a cosplay fundraiser?"

She taps her chin in thought. "You said the funds go to cystic fibrosis? I could be tempted into that, I have to admit. Plus, I've been working on a killer Maria Salazar."

Royer groans. "God, I'll bet you'll be perfect as Maria."

She blinks. "You know Maria?" *Deadly Class* is one of Darby's favorite comic book series.

"Yeah, my younger bro got me into it. She's one of my favorite characters. And you in... dayum."

"Easy, tiger," Darby says, but I can tell she's chuffed by the compliment.

"Hey, do you think maybe you could help me out with it?" Here it is—Royer's shooting his shot. "I mean, just so I get it right and appeal to the widest audience? I've never been to a con or cosplay anything. I don't want to do anything stupid."

Darby's skeptical expression thaws, and she nods after a beat. "Yeah, I might be able to help when I have time. I'm not planning the whole damn thing for you, though."

When I meet Cory's eyes, his expression is smug. But so is mine. Royer may be winning Darby over, but I'm definitely not falling prey to Cory.

Not now, not ever.

We spend the next hour sharing beers and discussing the DIK fundraiser. Darby and I are full of ideas on this topic, naturally, and Cory and Royer are attentive. At one point, Royer even pulls out his phone and starts taking notes. If you'd told me a month ago I'd be discussing cosplay with a frat guy, much less Cory Ingram, I'd have laughed in your face. But it's not so bad after all.

We leave tipsy and stroll across campus together.

"So you're a life sciences major, obviously, but which one?" Cory asks. He slows his pace, distance growing between the pair of us and Royer and Darby.

"Ecology." Our shoulders brush, and I'm all too aware of the heat rising from his tan skin. It's a little disorienting for someone whose only companion for months has been his hand.

"Cool, so do you want to be a park naturalist or something? Field ecologist? Environmental consultant?"

I tip a sidelong look at him, stunned he's familiar with career opportunities in my field. "Research and policy is my ultimate goal. I'm minoring in poli-sci."

"Think-tank stuff, hmmm." He casts an appraising glance over me that makes my heart beat faster and, once again, catches me off guard. "I can see it. What made you choose that?"

I dart another suspicious look at him. He's effortlessly engaging, and I imagine it's part of the reason so many people like him. All the more reason for me to be on guard. "I assume you're familiar with the Flint Water Crisis?" I ask, referencing the public health crisis involving the dangerous levels of lead in the municipal water supply.

Cory's eyes widen with alarm. "Holy shit, is that where you're from?"

"No, but my mom grew up in a small town in East Texas where something similar happened, back before people were paying much attention. She was diagnosed with Hodgkin's lymphoma when I was sixteen. It woke me up to the world around me, I guess, made me want to focus on things I could do to help make a difference."

"Wow." His forehead creases with sympathy. "I'm so sorry. How's she doing?"

"Okay. Fortunately, there are lots of medical interventions now that help, but it still sucks." The first few years after her diagnosis were especially rough and even now, despite that she's doing well, that feeling of being in limbo still sneaks up on me sometimes.

"No shit." His shoulder bumps mine again, and this time, I'm pretty sure it's on purpose. Part of me longs to melt against him. Freshman year of high school was the last time I had anything resembling a relationship. My mom's diagnosis sucked the emotional capacity from me for that kind of thing for a long while, and now I don't even know if I'm boyfriend material at all. Not that that matters with Cory. Still, I enjoy the brief contact more than I want to admit, along with the way his eyes crinkle at the corners when he meets my eyes. "That's a really noble cause, though. Very cool."

What's not cool is how much the regard in his tone affects me, making words jumble up on my tongue. I clear my throat. "I mean, I'm never gonna own a private jet, but I'm into it."

"Private jets are terrible for the environment anyway."

I crack a grin in spite of myself. "Your family totally has a private jet, right?"

"Yes." He hangs his head with a sheepish chuckle. "But my folks fund a whole bunch of carbon-offset programs, if that makes any difference."

"It doesn't hurt," I grant. I've only flown commercial a couple of times in my life. A private jet is a luxury I can't even imagine and reminds me how wildly different we are. That's probably a good thing.

Darby makes an abrupt exit into the house with a flash of a wave. Royer watches her back and then trundles toward me and Cory. "I have no idea how that went."

"She waved. It wasn't a total fail."

"I couldn't tell if it was a wave or if she was flipping me off."

"If she was flipping you off, believe me, she would've lingered to make sure you saw it," I tell him, unsure why I'm offering him any sort of reassurance in the first place. "Count it as a victory."

He screws up his face, then nods. "Alright. Guess I'll go." He thumbs in the direction of the frat house, leaving me alone with Cory. Dicey prospect that, because as my gaze roves his trim form, the strong jawline, his mouth, it occurs to me once more that he might not be so bad.

Then those lips I'm eyeing curl into a knowing smile. "It's okay to change your opinion of me, you know."

"It's okay to admit defeat." I huff out a laugh and move for the door of the house, punching in my code quickly.

I need out of his proximity, away from the warmth in his voice, that sheepish chuckle, and those dark eyes that look way too sincere for the party-boy persona I've ascribed to him.

I'M JUST CRAWLING INTO BED WHEN MY PHONE DINGS WITH A TEXT.

Hot Idiot: *Admit you had a decent time today.*

I knew I shouldn't have given him my phone number. Why isn't there a self-destruct mode for contacts?

Spencer: *I won't.*
Hot Idiot: *I know. But you don't have to. I could tell.*
Spencer: *Oh?*
Hot Idiot: *Yeah. If the way your chest was heaving when I pretended I was gonna kiss you wasn't enough, I caught you smiling. A lot. In fact, you might want to ice the corners of your mouth. Pretty sure they don't get worked out much that way. They'll probably be sore tomorrow.*

Wait. *Pretended* he was gonna kiss me? Bullshit. But if I make a stink about it, that'll just make him think I'm disappointed or hurt. Which I'm not. At all. Really.

Spencer: *You're an idiot. I smile plenty. There's just a reason you don't see it. (The reason is you, btw). Also, my chest was not heaving.*

We're not in a romance novel ffs. Chests don't heave. It was hot outside. I was simply breathing.
Hot Idiot: *It was heaving and it wasn't from the heat. You had goosebumps on the side of your neck.*

Goddammit.

Spencer: *We had a deal, remember? That means no more sitting next to me. No more parking in my spot. And definitely no more texting.*

And then, shockingly, he upholds his end of the bargain. The bubbles that signify he's typing something stop, then disappear without any further message.

Even more surprising is the disappointment that wraps around my gut as I snap my light off.

My window beckons me, but if he's upholding his end, then I'm gonna uphold mine.

No more watching him.

I kinda hate it already, but it's for the best.

10

CORY

At our chapter meeting on Sunday night, Royer announces the cosplay fundraiser idea, and the room goes dead silent, confused expressions lining nearly every member's face.

"Ummmm, is that like some subcategory of kink?" Dixon asks, "Because if so, I'm in, as long as no one's gonna whip the shit outta me."

"A hot girl can whip me any day," Jacobs says, smacking at the air with a grin.

A chuckle arises from the crowd, and Royer raises his hand for quiet. "Think of it more like... a costume party."

"Costume party, hell yeah!" Hannigan shouts. He never misses a chance to dress up. "Sounds way better than the beach theme last year."

"Fuck off, dude. That was an awesome party," Jacobs fires back. He planned the thing after all.

"We already live on the beach. What's so special about a beach theme?"

"I dunno, hordes of women in bikinis surrounding us?"

"Okay, point," Hannigan allows. "But this sounds badass."

Royer nods, relaxing under the encouragement. I knew he'd

been afraid to step outside our usual theme box. "It's gonna be super badass. We'll set it up like a con."

The con part causes more confused looks, so he then explains cosplay and cons in more detail, and the enthusiasm level goes from slightly intrigued to full-on excitement. Half an hour later, when we take a vote on it, it passes unanimously.

I catch Royer outside in the hall after the meeting, texting. He glances up at me. "I'm telling Darby we've settled on the theme and that I need her help figuring out some local businesses that might like to partner with us."

"Got her number, did ya?"

"Yeah, well, on the pretext that it's for cosplay stuff, but this counts, I'd say."

God, he's so gone for this chick. It's fascinating.

His phone dings, and he frowns at her reply. "She thumbs-upped my message."

"Harsh," I tease.

"Right? She might as well have said 'fuck you.'" He scowls at his screen.

"Or maybe she was just using it as it was intended and you're reading too much into it?"

"Nah, dude. The thumbs-up is snide. It's like hitting the 'like' button on Facebook. 'I am acknowledging your dumb post with complete ambivalence.' Get outta here with that shit. If you can't love something, don't bother. That's why Snap and IG are way better." He pockets his phone with a sigh. "Give up on ol' Crowe yet?"

"Nope. He had a good time with us. I can tell."

Royer bursts into laughter. "He looked like he was attending a funeral half the time."

"Yeah, yours." I chuckle. "Darby got some good digs in at you."

His cheeks redden. "Maybe at first. But then she settled down. Either way, I think you're gonna have to accept defeat on this one, dude. You've finally met the one person who has zero interest in you." He claps me on the back. "A good life lesson, probably."

"We'll see," I say, but the truth is, I haven't thought about the bet at all lately.

IN ANTHRO CLASS, I SLIDE INTO WHAT HAS BECOME MY USUAL SEAT next to Spencer, and he immediately frowns at me. It doesn't have the same scorn behind it that it has in the past, though. I take that as a positive sign.

I've come prepared, too. I unclip the pen he gave me from my collar and pass it to him. "Here's your pen back. Thanks so much, but I'm not in need of any performance enhancement yet." I did check the link out of curiosity over whether Spencer might have some issues in that department. As it turns out, the web address leads to a packet of other joke pens. Not gonna lie, I was both relieved and amused.

"Good for you, but I said you could keep it. Now, scram. This was part of our deal."

"I know, but I told you I absorb more sitting up here."

Spencer huffs out an "unbelievable," so I scoot one chair over. "Better? Now technically, I'm upholding my end. I'm not sitting next to you."

"You're infuriating."

"You're cute," I volley back, and I think I'm as startled as Spencer that the compliment just popped out of me like a verbal jack-in-the-box, but it's true. He's getting under my skin in a way that few have. Maybe even no one.

He wrestles back his bewilderment and presses his lips together. "Still not working."

"Still not doing anything," I lie. "I'm just a guy. Sitting in a class, trying to learn. Look, I won't even talk to you anymore." I make a lip-zipping gesture and face the front of the class as the professor walks in. From the back of the lecture hall, I'm almost certain I hear Royer snickering.

I listen to the lecture in silence, making notes. I don't speak to Spencer once. I don't even look at him, though I feel his eyes scrutinizing my profile a few times, and it's torture not to look over at him, too, or say something.

But I'm rewarded at the end of class when he's the one to lean toward me. "You didn't have to return the pen. It's a joke anyway, not a real place. I don't need performance enhancement, either." He sniffs as if to say, so there.

"I wasn't gonna judge, but good to know." I grab the pen and stuff it in my pocket. Fuck it, it's mine now. Then I stand and shoulder my backpack before dipping low, lips close to Spencer's ear in passing, and deal out my trump card. "I'm pretty sure you know I don't need any pills. Let's just say I'm aware that you've been keeping a close eye on me, and I don't hate it."

I don't wait for his reaction, though I'm dying to. I continue on out of the classroom, a blissful smile on my face.

God, that was satisfying.

Royer catches up to me outside, cracking up as he falls in step beside me. "What the fuck did you say to ol' Crowe, dude? His face went white as a ghost, then really fucking red. I thought his head might explode."

My smile widens. "Eh, I just let him in on a little secret."

11

SPENCER

Fuck my life. Fuck my measly, tired-ass life. Cory knows I've been watching him.

Or does he? Maybe he was just talking shit? Making a stab in the dark? I flip-flop back and forth between the two options, undecided, anxiety gnawing my gut. It's hard to say. But either way, if he really does know, I can't say I don't deserve being called out.

The part that threw me, though, was Cory saying he liked it. I reel back through my mind, mentally reviewing all the occasions I've watched him, trying to pinpoint when he might have figured it out.

Now that I think about it, did he start facing the window more often after he came to my room? When he fucked the silicone toy, was he totally aware that I was watching? Oh god. A shivery tingle runs up the insides of my thighs, and I'm in danger of popping a boner in full view of the entire quad as I remember how hot that session was. I'd jerked off to the memory of it for days and days, reluctantly wishing that ass had been mine.

No fucking way I can face him again now, though. Even if he said he liked it, how pathetic do I sound watching some dude jerk off through my window while jerking myself off, too?

I consider skipping our next class together, but what the hell am I going to do? Just skip the class the rest of the semester? And I can't drop the class now—it would completely wreck my schedule, plus it's past the refund period. So it sounds like I'm gonna be stuck in a mess of my own making until the end of the semester.

Annnnnd I've come full circle back to "fuck my life."

My head is a miasma for the rest of the day, and I'm even distracted during my shift at Shenanigans—that is, when I'm not keeping a wary eye out for Cory and his friends coming in. Maybe he'll put it on blast and tell everyone what I've been doing. Fuck, that would be too embarrassing to ever come back from. I'd have to drop out of school.

I'm grateful as heck when I finish my shift and am finally able to get back to my room, and my bed, where I plan to dive into the dark abyss of sleep for some peace. Tomorrow, I'll message Cory and apologize. And tell him I've stopped. It's the right thing to do.

My phone dings with a text as I'm shucking off my work pants, and I just know.

I try to gulp down the lump lodged in my throat that I'm pretty sure is my stomach as I flick the screen to life.

Hot Idiot: *Open your blinds.*

My thumb hesitates over the keypad. I could just not answer.

Hot Idiot: *I know you're there. I saw you walk into the house. And I can tell your light is still on.*
Spencer: *I'm really sorry. It won't ever happen again.*

Hot Idiot: *Lol*

LOL? What the heck does that mean? He doesn't believe me? He finds the whole situation funny?

While I'm puzzling over this, Cory calls me.

I wince as I answer. "Does LOL mean you don't accept my apology?"

Cory chuckles softly. "You're an interesting guy, Spencer." I don't know how to interpret that either, so I remain silent. "How long have you been watching me through the window?"

"I didn't..." I squeeze my eyes shut and exhale. "Not that long. A month, maybe. Shit. I know that's a huge violation of your privacy, and I'm so sorry."

"What all have you seen?" Cory sounds more curious than mad. I guess that's a hopeful sign?

"A lot," I say with another sigh.

"Tell me."

"God, okay. I've seen you getting dressed. Undressed. I've seen you with... ummm. Other guys."

"Not in a while," Cory says.

"Not recently, no. Just in the, in the past. Fuck, I'm so sorry," I say again. "And I'm not doing it anymore. I haven't done it since the whole truce thing."

"Because you didn't like it?"

"No! I mean, yes. Wait." I take a deep breath and try to compose my thoughts.

"So you liked watching me?"

"What?"

"You heard me." He pauses. "What did you think about when you were doing it? Did you get hard?"

My heart slams in my chest, pounding with a discombobulated mix of panic and arousal at the low timbre of Cory's voice. He definitely doesn't sound mad, but I'm not sure whether to trust that or not. Regardless, I decide to give him the truth. "Yes, I got hard. Ugh. That's such a huge violation of your privacy, and this is really fucking awkward."

Cory's laughter envelops me again. "How many times do I have to tell you I'm not mad? At all. I'm not mad, Spencer. Just curious. Did you jerk off while you watched me?"

"Yes." I've never in my life been so grateful for blinds so he can't see how ferociously I'm blushing. I feel the heat all the way to my toes.

"And what else did you see?"

"Specifically?"

"Specifically."

"I saw you jerking off once, and then there was the time with the—oh god—with the silicone ass." I groan.

"Mmmm, that was a good session," he purrs, and my dick twitches in response. I push it down. Bad timing, dick. Cory continues. "So you owe me, I'd say, wouldn't you?"

"I do? I mean... yeah, I guess, maybe? You're really not mad?" I will gladly wash his Jeep for the rest of the semester or tell him he can park in my spot. Fuck it.

"Right now, I'm horny as fuck, and I want the same show you got."

Wait. What? I stiffen in place, as if he's already watching me. "You want me to open my blinds and jerk off?"

"That's exactly what I want." The command in his voice makes my balls tingle and my aching dick even harder. I've never jerked off with an audience before, and when I consider it, or rather, consider doing it in front of Cory, the way my balls tighten says parts of me aren't opposed. "Open the blinds."

Goddammit. I have no idea what I'm going to find on the other side. Cory's entire frat mooning me? Making fun of me? Cory flipping me off? Cory... naked? Even considering the wretchedness of the current situation, the latter prospect still makes my stomach flutter.

With my heart still pounding, I flick my large overhead light off, leaving on my smaller desk lamp, cross the room, and yank the blinds up, accepting whatever my fate might be.

12

CORY

Spencer finally pulls the blinds up, giving me a view into his room and him standing in the middle of it, looking slightly panicked. Even in that bewildered state, I find him hot. He's as hard as I am, the erection tenting his boxers prominent.

"Touch yourself over your boxers," I tell him when he doesn't move. "Lemme see how hard you are."

Spencer exhales a quiet curse but does as I ask, smoothing a hand over the front of the fabric, then pulling it tight until I can see the outline of his stiff cock. Jesus fuck. The guy is packing, seriously packing, and I have to fight to keep my eyes from bulging out of my head.

"You're hung." I try to disguise the surprise in my voice, but I know he hears it because he snorts softly.

"You were making some assumptions, huh? Geeky guy? Tiny dick?"

"No. Sexy geek with probably an average dick like mine."

"Yours is not average."

"It's not a mule cock."

This time, he laughs. "Awww, does Cory Ingram have a case of penis envy?"

"I think I might," I admit and squeeze my dick, an answering crackle of pleasure racing up my spine. "Pull down your boxers and let me see it. Scientific interest."

Spencer hesitates for a long while before breathing out. "Okay." He drops the phone, picks it up, then manages to push his boxers down his thighs with one hand. His cock springs free and bobs heavily in the air.

"Jesus Christ, dude." Even in the dim lighting, I can tell a monster when I see one. I'm not a size queen by any means, but do I appreciate a smoking-hot specimen of cock? Absolutely. And damn do I wish I could see it up close. "Does the zoology department know there's a Kraken on campus?"

"Oh god." Spencer claps a hand over his face, fucking adorable, and lets it slide down. "Please stop."

"I'm not sure I can. It's large. Very fucking large."

"It is," he says matter-of-factly. "So should I put it away now?"

"I'm thinking no." Judging by his expression, that's not the answer he expected to hear, but I'm caring less and less about that now. "I'm definitely starting to get into the whole window stalker thing."

"I'm not a stalker!" Spencer protests vehemently, then lowers his voice. "I'm not a stalker. I just happened to be looking out the window once, and... why the hell are there no blinds on yours, by the way?"

"They got all fucked-up when Royer and Jackson were throwing Nerf balls at each other and Royer got tangled in the blinds, trying to keep from getting hit. Nearly broke the window and fell out. The replacements haven't come in yet."

"Doesn't the morning light bother you when you're hungover from late nights?"

I chuckle at the tangent. "I wear an eye mask."

"Cory Ingram wears an eye mask?"

I shrug. "They're comfy. And easy. You're being evasive." I tip my head in the direction of his crotch. "Touch it."

Spencer shakes his head. "No way. I don't think I can."

"Sure you can. Take that big-ass cock in your hand and stroke it while I watch." Not gonna lie, just bossing him around stokes my arousal.

Spencer's hesitation transmits through the glass, but after a long, long pause, he wraps a hand around his cock, eyes fluttering as he gives it a few strokes. I don't miss the soft groan that slips from his lips, either.

"Fuck yeah," I whisper, a tingle radiating from my balls, my dick twitching. "That's sexy. I totally get it. I can see you getting harder right before my eyes."

"I can't believe I'm doing this," he murmurs, eyes still squeezed shut, but his hand doesn't stop. He maintains that slow, steady pace, and I'm fucking aching to join him, to match him stroke for stroke. I've had plenty of sex, but I've never done anything like this, and it's honestly kinda blowing my mind. The only shitty part is the glass between me and him because I definitely, definitely want to see his cock up close now.

"Keep going," I encourage. "Pick up the pace if you want to."

"I do," he grits out, then squeezes his base just once before shuttling faster up and down his length. I wish I were closer, wish I could see the precum I'm sure is there, glistening on his head, wish I could flick my tongue over his fat crown and taste him. I unzip my shorts and tease my fingers over the head of my cock. "You like watching me too?" Some of the hesitation in Spencer's voice ebbs, and there's a gravelly, lust-drenched quality to it that makes me ache.

"Fuck yes. Get closer to the window. I wanna see you better." I do the same, rising from my chair so he can watch me as I move closer.

"Oh fuck, that's... god, it's even better this way."

For a few moments, we stand there, mirror images, stroking ourselves.

"What are we doing here?" There's a tight edge in Spencer's voice, and I'm not sure whether it's due to his hard cock or the rather unique situation we've found ourselves in.

I also don't care which it is at this point. I'm rock hard and dying to bust a load with him. "I'm pretty sure I'm about to get off to you getting yourself off."

Spencer groans. He's too far away from his little light for me to see much detail, which is a shame, but just the movement of his hand is enough. "Gonna come?" I grate out, and he nods before setting his phone on the windowsill. Then he wraps both hands around his cock, and my balls tighten, suddenly on the precipice of orgasm just from his shift in position.

"Fuck," I whisper into the phone as pleasure barrels up the length of my cock and it starts gushing. "*Fuckfuckfuck.*" Spurt after hot spurt spatters my hand, the floor, and I nearly drop my phone, managing to hang on to it at the last second and focus back on Spencer as I shudder and he loses it, too. It's too freaking dark to see it, but I can tell by how his shoulders jolt, his midsection contracts, and the shivery moans that come over the line before he stills.

"Bet admin didn't expect that kind of living and learning to be happening over there." I'm still breathless, pleasure ringing through me as I reach down to grab the nearest piece of cloth I can find to mop myself off.

Spencer exhales a tired, sated chuckle I've never heard, but fuck, it's adorable, too, and I wish it was in my ear. "Probably not, no." He turns his back to me, hunting around his room, returning as he wipes himself down, too. Then he picks up the phone again. "I'm not sure what I'm supposed to say now. Did that, ummm, satisfy my debt? This is really awkward."

"It doesn't have to be." I don't have to be right in front of him to know he's doing his little Spencer frown.

After a beat, he speaks again. "I suppose not, no. You're really not mad at me? I was almost certain I'd open the blinds and... I don't know." He sighs.

"I'm not mad at you. Told you I was into it. Though—" I edge closer to the window. "—I'm definitely not buying that you're not attracted to me now."

"I never said I wasn't attracted to you, just that I didn't like you. Those things can coexist. You're all about coexisting, going by the sticker on your Jeep."

Laughter bubbles out of me, and I swear I glimpse the tiniest smile on his face. I've seriously never met anyone like him. "Alright, fair point."

"God, I've never done that with anyone before. Like... just in front of someone that way."

"It felt good, though, right?"

"Fucking amazing."

"So you liked it."

He hesitates again. "Yeah, I liked it. Don't let it go to your head."

I have so many questions I want to ask. What he likes in bed. When the last time he had a boyfriend or regular hookup was? But I know better. "Soooo, since we're mutually attracted to each other and all, do you think you'd want to do this again sometime?" Preferably in person, but I'm not gonna push that issue, and besides, I'm more satisfied right now than I've been in a while, even if it was my own hand I was fucking.

"Maybe."

I'm gonna take that as a resounding yes.

13

SPENCER

I masturbated in front of Cory Ingram. Cory Ingram masturbated in front of me. While I watched openly. And then I came all over my window. That niggle of anxiety and shame over what I was doing has now become a cinema of filthy recollection. Cory's hand gliding over his cock, how I matched him stroke for stroke, the expression on his face as he came. The loads of cum shooting from his tip. It was hard enough maintaining my self-control before he was getting off to the sight of me doing the same. Dear god, what have we unleashed?

I hardly remember my classes the next day. My head is still swimming in the clouds, and even though I said "maybe" to doing it again, it's all I can think about. So much so that I almost overlook the fact that Cory sits beside me in anthropology our next class. Though, once again, he leaves a seat between us, like he's really upholding his agreement. But what's annoying about it today is that instead of finding it infuriating, I find it almost amusing. Almost.

After a simple "hey," Cory gets out his laptop and proceeds to... not ask me for anything. No pen or pencil requests, no "what did he just say?" of the professor when I know damn well he'd heard. Nothing.

Which means I sit in class, barely paying attention to the professor, surrounded by Cory's intoxicating scent, painfully aware of his fingers tapping on his keyboard as he takes notes and how differently they were moving the other night, what they might feel like moving on me.

This time, I'm the one who needs to ask what the professor just said, but I don't dare.

When class lets out, Cory packs up his stuff and then turns toward me as I do the same. "Want to study with me later at the library?"

"Nope," I tell him, even though I don't have a Shenanigans shift tonight, and even though I actually had planned to go to the library to work on a paper, and even though, fine, I kind of want to.

"Okay." He shrugs nonchalantly, then adds, "I'll be there from five to eight, usually near the carrels by the windows so I can gaze studiously out them and look like I'm pondering the meaning of life." He pulls a solemn expression and gazes off into the distance demonstratively, and I almost crack up before catching myself.

"Very distinguished." I shouldn't even be engaging him. Whatever.

"Not quite as distinguished as that load you shot all over your window last night, but I have aspirations," he teases, making my ears burn before he chuckles and skirts around me, leaving the lecture hall.

When I enter the library at six, I tell myself it's because I need a break from studying in my room, and because the library has a few resources that even the internet doesn't. It has nothing to do with Cory. At all.

As promised, he's got his stuff spread out at a table near the study carrels, and I bite back a grin when I see that he is, in fact, gazing out the window. He doesn't spot me as I draw closer, fully intending on taking one of the empty study carrels farther away from him until a small cellophane bag lying on the table catches my eye.

How in the hell?

I plunk my stuff on his table. "Where did you find those?"

Cory gives me a serene smile. "Hey, Spencer."

I point to the bag of Orange Sours. "Where? I've searched every gas station and grocery store between here and Timbuktoo. No one carries them. I've only ever found them at one store in Nacogdoches." And I'm pretty sure I'm the only reason the convenience store bothered to restock them.

"You can share mine, if you want. Why don't you have a seat?"

Remember earlier when I found him hot and almost amusing? I'm now back to infuriating. But I sit anyway, leaning over the table to turn the bag in my direction and make sure it's legit. It is. "Seriously, where did you find these?"

"I'm not telling. Trade secret."

"I swear to god, Cory Ingram."

"You were definitely doing a lot of that last night." He smirks and leans closer, breath warm on my cheek and orange scented. Seems he's been enjoying the candy himself. "And it was superhot." He nudges the bag toward me. "Here, have some. I'll share."

My willpower abandons me, and I reach into the bag, snagging a couple of the little orange candies and popping them in my mouth, my eyes falling shut as I barely stifle a moan. God, they're magic. Pure, terrible-for-you, artificially flavored, sugar-laden delight.

"Does Darby like flowers?" Cory asks when I return to the land of the living and reach for a couple more Sours.

"Not really. She's allergic to a lot of species."

"Candy?"

I narrow my eyes. "I'm not helping you do Royer's homework for him."

Cory considers me as I retrieve my books and computer from my backpack. "Oh, are you going to sit with me, then?"

"Yes. So I can annoy you the same way you do me in class."

"Annoy, huh? That's an interesting euphemism."

"It's not a euphemism."

"Okay." He shrugs lightly and goes back to his homework while I boot up my computer. I snatch up another handful of Sours, a tiny thread of guilt twining through me. "If Royer really wants to impress her, tell him to get her a Funko Pop or... a new manga or graphic novel. Something she's never heard of. And trust me, that'll be a challenge because she knows everything. She's super into BL stuff."

Cory taps out a message on his phone. "Perfect. Thanks."

Wait, shit. I just did exactly what I wasn't going to do.

We work in silence for a while. I fiddle with my paper, then check my email and frown before closing it out. Cory's gaze is on me again.

"Something wrong?"

"I'm just waiting to hear back about an interview for an internship this spring. It's really competitive and..." I have no idea why I'm telling him this, except that he happens to be there and I need to vent. "One of my profs forgot to send their rec. I got that squared away, but now I'm worried I won't get an interview anyway."

"What kind of internship is it?"

"Environmental policy research. It's probably one of the toughest internships to get as a life sciences major and probably sounds kinda boring, but you get to do fieldwork, too, and it's one of the best pipelines for a new college grad into the big think tanks."

"I'm familiar." Cory smiles. "My uncle is on the interview board."

"Who's your uncle?"

"Peter Bayliss."

I stare at him in awe. "No shit? How did I not know this?" Bayliss is an FU grad and was a founding member of the Global-Watch Institute in the nineties. He still sits on the board and also teaches a single upper-level class on biodiversity conservation that I'm dying to get into next year as a senior. Heck, he's a big reason I applied to FU in the first place.

"You never ask me any questions." Cory gives me a pointed arch of his brow. "You're always too busy trying to ignore me or staring longingly at me while trying to deny you actually like me."

"We've been over this. I can find you attractive and not like you at the same time." He has a point about the questions, though, and possibly the part about denying I like him. Man, maybe I am a bit of a dick, too. But doesn't that make us even?

"Well, since you're not going to ask, my uncle is how I got into sailing and fishing and stuff. He used to take me out on his boats when I was a kid because my parents were always wrapped up in some project or another, building the firm and whatnot." Cory looks over at the window again. "And now I get to continue the legacy. Yay." He makes sarcastic jazz hands. "That's awesome you're going for that internship, though."

I feel like I should say something in response to that, but it's not like I'm his best friend or anything. We're just two guys who jerk off in front of each other.

"Anyway," he dismisses the topic with a smile. "So when did you get into cosplay?" There he goes again with his questions.

"High school. I was big into it freshman year here. That's how I met Darby. A campus cosplaying meet-up. But I don't get to go much these days. My course load plus work just... I dunno, sapped my willingness to put in the effort," I say, relieved for the change of subject.

"Oh. That blows."

I laugh. "That's life. I know it's unimaginable to someone like you to sacrifice a hobby in the name of staying in school."

His brows flicker together, and I can tell the barbed comment has landed. I refuse to feel bad about it, though, because it's true.

"You said you did it a lot freshman year, and now you don't. So something changed. Did you lose a scholarship or something?"

Damn, he's sharper than I give him credit for. This time, it's my brows knitting. "I still have a partial scholarship, but my folks were originally helping with the rest. They wanted me to have the American Dream-type of college experience they didn't have. But Mom had a setback with the lymphoma the summer after freshman year. She and my dad—he works in a mill—had to reduce their work hours. Money got tight, and I can't stand the idea of taking any more of it from them, so I pay my own way now."

Cory's gaze softens. I know that look, and I don't want his pity, so I put the spotlight on him, trying for a light tone. "So disc golf, fraternity, your folks own one of the biggest advertising firms in the US. That's where you're heading after you finish college, right?"

Cory nods slowly, still seeming a little distracted. "Yeah. I like advertising. I'm good at it. Seems like the natural progression of things. I'm all for it, except my folks want me to start in NYC, and I really don't want to leave California. I love it here." He glances down at his hands, seeming suddenly self-conscious. "Sounds so dumb to say aloud. It's a dream job most people would die for, especially in this economy and especially after hearing about your folks. And here I am bitching about having to leave Cali?" He laughs softly. "Sometimes I just wish I could work on a fishing boat all day. See, who says I haven't made any sacrifices?"

I bark out a laugh. "A fishing boat? Really? Cory Ingram on a fishing boat. Have you ever even been on anything other than a fancy yacht?"

He grins, eyes alight with amusement. "I spent last summer working on a fishing charter. I fucking loved it, and it paid absolute shit."

I'm floored imagining Cory on a fishing boat, reeling in fish, cleaning up fish guts, and it's his turn to laugh. "It's true. Ask my parents. They hated it. Wanted me to go intern in NYC, which I guess I'm gonna do this summer."

Cory's lack of enthusiasm has me giving him a longer look, but before I can ask further, he leans back in his chair, folds his arms over his chest, and gives me one of those looks that says I'm about to be judged. "So have you been sailing since you've been here?"

This man thinks I have time for sailing? I snort. "Fuck no."

He barks out an incredulous laugh. "Are you serious? That's a crime. I mean, Jesus, dude, they have an intro to sailing course here. It's practically a requirement."

"I took intro to marine biology instead. The time slot was better for the rest of my schedule, and it made more sense for my major."

"An ecology major living in southern California who doesn't

know how to sail and has never been out on a boat? I don't know. Better not mention that to anyone," he teases, then sobers. "I could take you out sometime."

My heart instinctively gallops at the thought of an afternoon on a boat with Cory, but I shake my head. "Nope. I'm good. Thanks." Despite showing up at the library in the first place, I'm still firmly in the camp of reducing the amount of time I spend with him. I think.

"Right." His gaze drifts to the window again. "Fair enough. Just tell me when you want to go."

"Sure." I roll my eyes. "I'll pencil that in for after I graduate."

With a shrug, he turns back to his computer. I read through my paper one last time, marking it up with the red pen I bought for this purpose. I try to ignore the thrill that goes through me when I sense he's watching me, try to ignore the way his face lights up when I take a break to eat a few more Sours or to grab my laptop and pore over the internet for some new research. Try to ignore the sound of his phone buzzing every few minutes with messages from his nine million friends. Mostly, I try to ignore the fact that even though I choose not to talk to him much, I still enjoy his presence.

Shit. I think I'm in trouble.

At eight, Cory closes his laptop. "I'm gonna head out. I've got a thing."

"Yeah, I'm going too." Of course he's got a *thing*. I've got a single bed and a fish tank. But my eyes are growing heavy, and bed sounds good.

The dark sky overhead unleashes a torrential downpour just as we exit the library. I jump back under the awning with a muttered curse. That's alright. A lot of times, these rain showers disappear as quickly as they come.

"Care to share my umbrella?"

Black nylon barrels toward me with a whoosh, stopping two

inches from my nose as I flinch backward. Cory lifts the umbrella, all chiseled jaw and pretty white teeth.

"No, thanks. I'll just wait it out." Why the heck didn't I think to check my weather app?

Cory tips his head toward the sky. "You're gonna be waiting a while."

"I'm patient." A fat raindrop plops onto my forehead, and I shrink against the wall of the building.

His laugh is deep and smooth, as rich in melody as his eyes are dark. "No, you're not, and you're gonna get soaked. C'mon, is the prospect of sharing an umbrella with me really so bad?"

It's not that it's bad, just that it seems a little dangerous.

I gaze out at the quad and its smattering of people with umbrellas and ponchos that glisten under the lamps strung along the sidewalks, along with plenty of folks who just don't care and are jumping and dancing around in the quickly-forming puddles.

"Okay," I answer resignedly, then step under the umbrella when he makes room for me. We dart from beneath the awning and start across the quad, sidestepping puddles. "You didn't sound very excited to go to NYC this summer. Do you have to go?" I ask, curiosity getting the best of me. I would've thought Cory would be all about big-city life.

"Eh. My parents let me play around freshman and sophomore year, but I don't think it'll fly anymore now that I'm closer to graduating." He lapses into thoughtful silence, sucking on his lower lip. "But I think about it. I came to college wanting what they have, wanting to put my mark on something like they have, wanting to be some media bigwig or CEO, make a big splash, walk into a room full of people and command attention like they do. Now, I don't know. They work 24/7, 365. They have a winter house in Telluride, a loft in Minneapolis. Boats in marinas in San Diego. A jet. And I can't think of the last time they've used any of them for recreation. They eat, sleep, and breathe advertising, and I know that's my future. I know I'll be fine at that. And besides, how shitty-privileged-white-kid does it sound to be discontent with all of that? But I can't help it. Sometimes I want more... life. Time to go fishing if I want. Disc golf, all the things you mentioned before." He shrugs. "I dunno, or maybe I just need to grow up. Real sacrifice. Like you said."

For the first time, I want to disagree with him not just because he's Cory, but because watching his expression as he says all of that makes me feel genuine sympathy for his position.

I need to nip that inclination in the bud before I do something stupid like decide he might actually be a decent human with more depth than I anticipated.

"Maybe," I demur as we come to a stop outside the LaL house. "But maybe there's a workaround, too. You don't have to work the way your parents work. Maybe you can figure out how to carve out time for yourself and the things you enjoy doing."

"Says the guy who no longer has time to cosplay." Cory adjusts the umbrella, angling it with the breeze so we don't get spattered. "That little smirk of yours says I've made my point."

"I'll admit no such thing," I say with a twist of a smile.

"I know. You're a tough one, Spencer Crowe." He digs in the side pocket of his backpack and, magically, comes up with another bag of Sours. Is he stockpiling them? He waves it under my nose. "For the road."

I eye them for a moment, considering not taking them, but fuck it, I want them. I want a lot of things right now. "Thank you."

Cory grins. "That was the most begrudging thank-you I've ever heard. You're welcome." He bows with a flourish, then hands me his umbrella. "Keep this, too."

"But—"

"I've got plenty of other ones." He ducks into the patter of rain, and I watch his long-legged, unhurried stride to the DIK house, shoulders of his tee darkening in the downpour while a wistful ache unfurls in my chest.

A few moments after he disappears around the corner of the house, my phone pings.

Hot Idiot: *I'd like to see you in the window again tonight.*
Spencer: *Is this a transactional thing now? You gave me candy and an umbrella, so I owe you another show?*
Hot Idiot: *Nope, just something I really want. You don't have to do anything. Ever.*
Hot Idiot: *Or... You can just watch me.*

Goddammit.

14

CORY

I'm drowning in costume ideas. Spider-Man, Superman, Batman, He-Man... so many "mans." Even Halloween doesn't get as much consideration as I've given the DIK cosplay fundraiser—or DIKcon, as we've started referring to it—but the whole frat has gotten into the theme. Hell, Royer's talking about ordering handmade shit off Etsy to complete his Witcher costume, probably trying to impress Darby, and I still have no clue what I'm going as. I just know I don't want to be the dude with a shitty low-effort costume.

I spin my laptop toward Spencer so he can see my ideas. He shows up with increasing frequency at the library when I'm there and he doesn't have another class or Shenanigans shift.

"You created a whole Pinterest board?"

"Yeah, gonna judge me for that? Pinterest is handy."

His mouth quirks at one corner. He's amused. I like an amused Spencer. He's prickly in general, but there's no doubt I'm seeping under his usual anti-frat-boy armor. In class, he no longer complains when I sit by him, and he'll actually greet me now. When he joins me in the library, I always have a bag of Orange Sours waiting for him. He's started talking about himself more, too, his life, his parents back in Texas, and asking me about what I've got going on. Sometimes he seems to catch himself not disliking me and tries to reel himself back in, but I know better.

And then there are our window sessions, which have also increased in frequency, and I'm definitely not complaining about that, either.

So all in all, operation Get Spencer In My Bed is looking promising... except my own motivations are starting to get mixed up. I came into it with a conquest mindset, and now? I don't know, I just like the guy. And I definitely, definitely still want him.

I eye him as he scrolls through my board, brows flickering together in concentration. Goddamn, he's cute. Cute and sexy at the same time, and just watching him scroll my board gets me hot. His teeth rake over his lower lip, and I almost groan. I'm dying to touch him, kiss him, put my hands on him for real.

Assessment complete, his gaze flickers toward mine again, then rakes over me. "Honestly? You could pull off any one of these and make it amazing."

"I know that wasn't an actual compliment."

"Of course not," he says, pressing his lips together, though I can see the smile beneath. "Purely scientific assessment."

"I'm kinda partial to Batman or the Joker. So where would I start in pulling that all together? Costume shop?"

He nods thoughtfully. "Yeah, and there's a rental place in town, too, but they've got more period pieces than modern stuff." He gnaws on his lower lip and, after another glance at his computer screen, closes the top. "I know a place we could go right now if you wanted to check it out? They do both rentals and purchases."

"Are you asking me on a date?" When I feign shock, he snort-laughs. It's kind of a dorky sound I've grown annoyingly fond of.

"No, I just can't in good conscience let you bastardize the DC universe. What kind of cosplay geek would I be?"

"Of course not. You have a reputation to uphold, and I clearly need a guide, so lead the way."

We take my Jeep, Spencer telling me when to turn in between tilting his head back and letting his eyes fall shut in the late-afternoon sunlight. The wind whips our hair into ridiculous disarray as we drive, leaving us cracking up at each other at stoplights. It's a gorgeous afternoon, and I take a moment to acknowledge that the warm, glowy feeling in my chest might just be contentment.

We stop outside a squat stucco building with a hand-painted sign reading The Enchanted Masque. I had no idea it was here. Usually, I just grab my Halloween costumes from a big-box shop and call it done since I've always been more into getting the costume off later with someone else than putting it on.

Bells on the door chime as we enter. There are one or two other folks milling around, but it's otherwise quiet. An older fella stands behind the counter and lifts his hand to us. "Hey, Spence. Long time, no see."

"School, work. Rinse, repeat," Spencer explains with an affable grin that still catches me off guard when it makes a rare appearance.

The guy nods in understanding. "Let me know if you need help with anything."

The shop appears to be divided into sections, period costumes up front, more standard prepackaged costumes lining the left side and back. Spencer directs us toward them.

"Why does he get to call you Spence and I don't?"

"Because I like him." Spencer cuts me a mischievous look sidelong before stopping in front of a rack of costumes. "Here we go. So, you can start with a kind of basic base layer and add on personal touches to get a more realistic effect. Some people even have custom weapons made, and you'll see plenty of folks who will take a costume and add a lot more detail than what's typically included."

"What all have you cosplayed?" I ask as we flip through the racks, pausing here and there in front of different costumes. Some are your average cheapo costumes in a plastic bag, but some are more intricate, with a price tag that reflects the handiwork.

"Gah. A lot. I've done Batman before, but I don't really have the build for it. Spider-Man is a really fun one because he's a little leaner, like me, so it's not such a stretch. Link from The Legend of Zelda. I tend to stick more mainstream. Darby gets more creative."

"I'd love to see you as Spider-Man." It slips out, but it's true. Spencer in a Spider-Man costume sounds mouthwatering. My gaze drifts lower, toward his package, and Spencer hooks a finger under my chin, guiding it back up.

"Quit it. I know what you were thinking."

"Can't help it." I grin. "Any windows nearby?"

He swats me, hiding his smile as usual, and reaches into the racks, pulling out a Joker costume. "Want to pick a few to try?"

We end up in the dressing rooms, arms weighted down with entire comic universes. I waggle my brows. "You can come in with me if you want."

"I'll stay out here," he says resolutely, dropping onto a settee.

I take my pile of costumes into the dressing room and work through them slowly, showing him every one. Mario and the Mad Hatter are first. Mad Hatter is just too much costume, though, and makes me sweat. We both crack up at the Mario one, but I nix it since I've worn a Mario costume to a previous DIK party before. Tony Stark and Mad Max go into the "maybe" pile.

Next is the Dark Knight, and Jesus, there are a lot of pieces. Once I get the base layer of leatherlike spandex on, I poke my head out the door. "I need your help with the rest of this. I'm not sure where all the pieces go."

"You could just look at the picture," he says but is on his feet and pushing in behind me a second later. We snap and fasten a couple of accessories in place. Arm braces, some embellishment that goes over my quads.

Spencer assesses me in the mirror from behind as I hold up a codpiece. "What do you think? Is this the one?" As I fiddle with the codpiece, Spencer's gaze shoots down, and he swallows visibly.

"You make a very, very good Dark Knight. Hang on." Gently, he reaches up and pulls the eye mask down over my face, eyes still fixed on my reflection in the mirror. "Wow, yeah. This might be the one. Your jawline..." He trails off.

I preen over the compliment. "I should rewatch the movie and see if there's anything else I can add on." Spinning around to face him, I try to come up with some movie quote, but the intensity in his expression stops me in my tracks.

"No. I mean yes, you could definitely add on." His chest rises and falls more rapidly. "Like, whatever. You could add anything on."

I tilt my head, eyeing him. "This getting to you?"

"No." He shakes his head rapidly. "Totally fine over here, yeah. Yeah, fine."

He's so lying, and wow, wish I'd known earlier that a man in costume is a Spencer Crowe cheat code.

"Sure?" I take a step closer "So you definitely wouldn't want me to kiss you right now? Just like you definitely didn't want me to kiss you when we were playing disc golf?"

"Yes. I mean no. I mean... maybe?" He grabs the codpiece from my hand. "Gimme that."

"You going to put it on for me?"

He glances down, blushing when he realizes what he's holding before steeling his jaw. "Sure, no big deal." He presses it to my crotch, where my boner is comically obvious. "Um." Another swallow. Have I mentioned lately that he's cute?

His gaze lifts to mine. Our lips are close, then closer, until I can feel the heat of his breath and the soft sigh that he exhales when I brush my lips over his. They're soft and warm, and when I flick my tongue out to taste the lower, he splays a palm against my chest, wrapping the fabric, and for a second, I wonder if he's about to push me away.

Then he pulls me closer, our mouths sealing firmly, his tongue gliding against mine, the taste of him sparking an inferno inside me. Fuck, somehow kissing him is even better than getting off with him in front of a window, and that's a first for me, but I'm not going to question it. I skim my hands up his side, his shoulders, his lower back, registering how he arches into me, presses against me, all tight body and thick cock that asserts its presence along my inner thigh.

"You realize you're still holding my crotch, right?" I murmur with a soft chuckle when we break for air.

"Right." He lets the codpiece clatter to the floor, and I urge him back against the dressing room wall. The friction when I roll my hips against him is too much, not enough. Both at once. Spencer's hands anchor around my hips, keeping me moving until he lets out a quiet moan. "Is this the best place to be doing this?" he rasps.

My brain isn't working properly, so I just nod, eyes on his, searching for any hesitation or resistance as I coast a hand down his chest, over his abdomen, until I reach the fastener on his shorts and undo it. His breath leaves his lungs in a hushed groan as I reach inside and wrap my hand around the length of him. Rock hard and throbbing with his rapid pulse and an alluring heat. "I've been wanting to touch you for so fucking long," I confess.

"Oh shit," he whispers when I begin stroking him slow and easy, getting a feel for his shape, relishing the drops of precum that bead from his slit and glide under the pad of my thumb.

He's fumbling while I stroke him, and I adjust, yanking off the chest piece so he has access to the waistband of my costume, where his fingers brush over my straining hard-on. I have to bite back a loud moan, dampen it by sinking my teeth into my lower lip when he starts stroking me, too. I rest my forehead against his, our breaths colliding, eyes locked as pleasure builds in steady increments.

"I want to taste you," I tell him and again watch him, wary of any hesitation, even if I think it might kill me to stop.

He nods rapidly, garbling something that I think is a "fuck yes."

Good enough for me.

I drop to my knees, yanking his shorts down. His thighs flex underneath my palms as I slide them up, using one to grip his base and steer his cock to my lips. I want to savor this, certain I've never sucked a cock as mouthwatering as Spencer's thick erection. I lave my tongue over his crown, eyes fluttering shut at my first taste of him and the choked noise he makes in response.

I've been harboring a growing suspicion that touching Spencer would prove addictive. Now, for better or worse, I know for sure.

15

SPENCER

One of FU's most popular guys is on his knees, sucking my dick in a dressing room while wearing a Dark Knight mask. I can't believe this is even happening and keep wondering whether I somehow slid into some parallel universe where we've reversed lives and I'm Mr. Social Animal while he's the science nerd.

My skin tingles as he kisses the tip of my cock, then sucks it into his mouth, teasing me with his tongue and the pressure of his lips.

Fisting my hands in the soft strands of hair curling out from his mask, I can't stop watching him as he dips lower, licking from base to shaft before engulfing me so suddenly I have to grit my molars to stifle a cry.

These past few weeks that we've been watching each other in the window have built up a slow but desperate ache inside of me, a craving that I kept telling myself I had no interest in satisfying. But I've been lying to myself, and never has it been more obvious than now, as the heat of his mouth scorches me and sends me spiraling into bliss with every second that passes.

He pauses, glancing up at me. I'm not sure what he's

checking for, but I've noticed him doing it more lately. Is it consent, interest? Curiosity? His gaze is hooded behind the mask, pupils dark and wide, and the only thing I can do is nod fervently—a yes that my lips can't seem to remember how to speak.

He rumbles a soft, pleased sound that curls my toes, his fist tightening, pace slowing like he means to draw this out into the sweetest torture possible.

It's working, though. Tingly pressure ebbs and flows at the base of my spine, and I let go of his hair to brace a palm against the wall behind me when my thighs start to quiver.

"Cory, I can't..." I rasp, and he stops immediately, that searching gaze sweeping over me again. "Wait, no, don't stop," I whisper. "I meant I'm gonna... I'm close."

A knowing smile spreads over his lips, and he chuckles quietly. "So you don't want me to stop?"

Part of me wants to smack him in that moment because he knows exactly what he's doing, but the other part of me finds the mischief in his eyes so alluring that I don't even care. "I don't want you to stop," I confess before he can tease me more.

Three more expert strokes of his hand, his mouth wrapped around the head of my cock, and I sink my teeth into my lower lip, holding back a cry as my body locks up with tension and then releases. My orgasm explodes out of me, a momentary out-of-body experience that makes my eyes roll back in my head. I'm vaguely aware that he keeps going, wringing every last drop from my dick until I start to sag against the wall. He lets me slide from his mouth only to grip my hips and steady me.

Sinking back on his heels, he swipes at his mouth with the back of hand, amusement dancing in his eyes. Before I can ask what he's so smug about—as if I really need to, anyway—he surprises me.

"You're fucking gorgeous, Spencer Crowe."

Not what I expected, and it leaves me speechless. I extend a hand to help him rise with an awkward glance at his straining erection. "Let me."

He shakes his head with a smile. "You don't have to. This isn't tit for tat. I just wanted to do that."

"It's not?" I realize I sound like an idiot, but here I am, blown off-kilter by a guy I've had to fight increasingly hard to dislike, or at least be bored by.

"I wanted to," he reiterates, which doesn't at all calm the butterflies in my stomach. "I like you, even if you say you don't like me—which I still think is a total lie, by the way."

"You're okay, I suppose."

Cory cracks up. "So I've worked my way up to 'okay'?"

"Keep up the good work and you might approach 'alright' by the end of the year."

He makes a face. "'Alright' is the same thing as 'okay.'"

"It's slightly better than okay."

Before we can get into the semantics, Cory brushes a searing kiss over my lips that gets interrupted by a knock on the door.

"Just checking that everything's okay in there, gents," Mr. Featherman says.

My cheeks flame, but Cory, smooth as ever, has it covered. "All good. Spence was just helping me with the fit of this costume."

"It's perfect. We'll be out in a second." I try to rub the heat from my cheeks. Doesn't work when Cory's grinning at me like a loon. I swat him.

"Great, I'll ring you up when you're ready."

We wait until his footsteps recede, and Cory laughs.

"Stop." I swat him again. "He totally knows."

"He totally knows, yeah. Now, help me get out of this thing."

Once Cory is back in his street clothes, we straighten the dressing room and leave the extra costumes piled neatly on a chair. He shoves me out of the dressing room with a smack to my ass. "Get that hot ass outta here."

I scoff, even as his compliment resonates inside me far more than I want it to. "If you're trying to get me to tell you you're hot in return, I'm not going to. You hear it on a daily basis."

"Not from you," he counters with an affable grin. Asshole.

"You're fishing."

"I do love fishing. And I told already you I'd take you out sailing—or fishing—anytime."

We've gone from costumes to a dressing room blowjob to fishing all in a span of ten minutes. Something about that strikes me as funny, and I can't help the laughter that breaks free.

"What?" Cory wears a clueless expression, and I wave a hand, trying to calm down. A bigger smile curves his lips. "Wow, I don't think I've ever heard you laugh. I didn't know you were capable of it."

"I laugh!"

"Not like this. Usually, it's this sort of sarcastic snort-laugh."

"Laughs can't be sarcastic."

"Like hell. You're living proof, trust me."

That makes me laugh again, this time less hysterical sounding. I'm more relaxed and at ease than I've been in a long time, and god, it feels nice. "See?" I point out. "I laugh. I even smile sometimes, too. I'm a real people person."

"Uh-huh." He rolls his eyes.

"You don't believe me? I'll have you know that I'm charming." That adjective has never been applied to me in my life that I can recall.

"Uh-huh. The way you yelled at me the first time I ever met you was the most charming experience of my life."

"I'm not sure sarcasm over whether I'm charming or not works here considering you just blew me in a dressing room while wearing a Dark Knight mask." Jeez, talk about things I never expected to happen.

"Fair point."

"And don't call me Spence."

"Damn." He digs for his wallet as we approach the front counter. "I thought I snuck that one by you."

"Hardly."

Cory pays for his costume, and we have just enough time to grab an In-N-Out burger before I have to get to my Shenanigans shift. I don't know how I'm going to get through it without wearing a stupid, lust-drunk grin the whole time.

"So, would you want to do that again sometime?" he asks when he drops me off outside the LaL house, Jeep idling behind my parked car.

"It's a possibility," I concede, biting back a smile as I slide from the seat.

"Oh yeah, I'm definitely moving up to 'alright' before the end of the week."

I give his smirk a dismissive wave of my hand, but even that seems forced. The truth is I do like him. Enough that it makes me nervous. Enough that I worry I won't be able to stop thinking about him. "Don't count your chickens before they hatch."

"Bok bok," he crows, and I shake my head with a laugh. He's still an idiot. But a really charming one.

DARBY SWISHES A CARROT STICK THROUGH SOME HUMMUS, A PRIM smile playing over her lips as she continues to ignore the pointed stare I turned on her the second we set our lunch trays down in the dining hall.

This calls for escalation. I push my sandwich aside and rest my elbows on the table, concentrating the full intensity of my gaze upon her until she cracks up. "Oh my god, what is it?"

"Chance says Royer was at the house last night. In your room. With the door closed. Spill, you secretive little minx."

She stabs a carrot stick toward me, and I open my mouth chomping it as she laughs. "It was nothing. Really. We were just going over some con ideas and he was telling me about his costume. Besides," she gives me the same accusing stare, chin down. "Selena says she's seen you and Cory at the library a couple of times, so who's the close-lipped little minx now?"

I can't help it, I break into a grin. Guilty as charged. "Touché, but you're still evading. I'll spill if you will."

"Finnnnnne. Will is pretty okay." Darby wipes her fingers off on a napkin, then balls it up and sets it aside. "More down to earth than I gave him credit for, and there may have been a moment. You know, a *moment*, the other night."

"You're giving me a dreamy smile right now. Was there smooching? Hanky-panky? Fluids exchanged?"

She thwaps me. "That's not a dreamy smile, dammit. And no, no fluids exchanged, hanky-panky, or smooching. Yet. But almost, and I think I would, but..." She trails off, fiddling with a lock of brown hair.

"Darby, that was in eighth grade. I think it's safe to let the whole dance thing go. Don't people deserve second chances?"

"You tell me, Mr. Canoodles-with-Cory-Ingram-in-a-library."

"We're not canoodling." I busy myself with my sandwich wrapper. "Just studying."

She prods my lower lip with a grin. "You're doing the dreamy smile now!"

"Stop," I say, but we're both laughing again before I sigh. "Okay, maybe I was a little too harsh on Cory. I..." God, exactly how much do I confess? No way I'm going to tell her about our window sessions. Way too private. "We hooked up in a dressing room at The Enchanted Masque the other day. And Darby, you can't tell anyone!" I tack on hurriedly as she crows in delight.

She puts a hand over her heart. "I swear I won't. Holy shit, Spence that's so... unexpectedly scandalous of you. And those dressing rooms are tiny."

"I know," I reply with a wicked grin.

She seems to have forgotten her food entirely now. "So, was it good? Does he live up to the hype?"

"I'm afraid so." Now I know I'm in dopey smile territory, because my lips tingle just thinking about his kiss, and my skin hums with the memory of his hands on me. We got caught before I could go down on him, but now I'm desperate to, desperate for more of him in any capacity, really. I need to come back to earth, though. "But I'm trying not to make a big deal out of it." The flutter I get in my stomach just thinking his name suggests I'm a hypocrite. "I don't know where it's going, probably nowhere, knowing Cory."

"Probably smart," she nods, which is enough to bring me back to earth. "I'm doing the same. DIKs will be DIKs, right?" She sounds hesitant, though, which tells me she's definitely more into Royer than she's going to let on. "We can still have some fun, though, right?"

"Right." Fun. Something I haven't had in a long time. That's all.

16

CORY

Shenanigans is slammed for open-mic night, and the DIKs have taken up at least half of Spencer's section. He seems harried when he drops off our third round of drinks, and by the time he arrives with a tray on his shoulder, fully laden with what looks like half of the restaurant's happy-hour specials, he's downright bedraggled, hair mussed, cheeks flushed.

I want to grab him, sneak him into a dark corner, and kiss him until the tension in his shoulders eases and he melts against me. It's such a weird, unexpected feeling that's been throwing me since the dressing room at the costume shop last week. We've kissed a few more times since then, still hang out at the library when he can, and he gave me a blowjob in one of its bathrooms two days ago that still makes my dick hard when I think about it. It's unlike me to be so hung up on a guy. I've not been in a relationship since high school, and I feel rusty as fuck. I don't assume we're dating, but we're very definitely hooking up, and I very definitely wouldn't mind more.

Spencer deals out baskets of fries and wings like cards, perfectly efficient, and when he gets to my order, I peel away from the convo the other guys are having about the last Kings' game and closer to him. "I didn't know there'd be so many of us, sorry."

"Don't worry about it. It's my job." He ticks his chin toward my almost empty glass, all business. Yeah, he's definitely stressed. "Want another?"

"Yes, please."

When he gives my polite request some side-eye, I grin and sneak a hand under the table, skimming it along the side of his thigh, and there it is, the reluctant Spencer smile.

He quells it immediately and gives me a stern look, speaking softly. "Stop that."

"Then stop looking so stressed. Want me to put a fifteen-minute ban on anyone ordering anything else? Give you a little break?"

"You going to fold my laundry next? Seriously, I can handle this." He rolls his eyes, but I catch the return of his smile. "Now, quit badgering me so I can keep doing my job."

"Did you hear back about the interview yet?" He was worrying about it again the other day at the library. I like to think I distracted him well enough with my cock, though.

His smile full-on blossoms at the question. "Yeah, I got one. Friday."

"Dude! That's great!" I'm pumped for him, though not surprised. He's easily one of the smartest guys I've met, and the way his eyes are alight spreads a warm joy through my chest.

"I know. I can't believe it. I thought with all the candidates and then my issue with the recs—"

"Spencer!" someone barks from behind, and he snaps to attention, whisking up empty bottles and glasses from the table.

"I gotta go."

"Go, yeah. But I want to hear more about it later."

I turn my attention back to the table and narrow my eyes at Javi's stare.

"Still haven't landed him yet, have you? Jesus, what happened to you, dude?"

"I will," I toss out, reacting on pure instinct and sheer competitiveness and immediately feeling a leaden weight of guilt in my gut. Why did I even say that?

Royer gives me a funny look but doesn't comment, so I turn my attention to my food, hoping Javi will just forget about it.

"So what's the real story on Spencer?" Royer asks me an hour later. He and I are the only ones left at the table, and I'm sucking down water since I've got an early class tomorrow. "You've been a ghost lately, and I know your ass isn't *that* big of a fan of the library."

"I like him. He's not what I expected."

"Yeah? Gonna lock it down?" He arches a brow. "I don't think I've seen you serious about someone in… ever."

"Because I haven't been since I got here. I'm not sure I even remember how to. Like, do I ask him if he wants to be my boyfriend? That sounds stupid." I chuckle.

"Yeah, don't say that. Maybe something like, 'do you wanna be exclusive?'" Royer wrinkles his nose. "That sounds just as dumb. Shit, I guess I'm out of practice, too." He scratches his jaw. "When I was seeing Erika, I can't remember how it got brought up. I think I told her I was really into her and didn't want to see anyone else, and she said the same." Erika was Royer's freshman-year girlfriend. She bailed right before summer, saying she wanted to expand her horizons and have a hot-girl summer. Royer had been a total mope for the rest of the summer until he landed himself a threesome at the DIK's back-to-school mixer. "I don't think that would work with Darby, though," he muses.

"How's that going?" He's right; I haven't seen much of him lately. I'm totally out of the loop where he's concerned, too.

"She tolerates me now. Sometimes she smiles. I got her to tentatively agree to go to DIKcon with me."

I laugh. "Are there certain terms that need to be met?"

"Yeah, she says my costume can't look stupid." He rolls his eyes, but he's grinning. "She's not gonna have to worry about that, though. I'm gonna look badass. And—" He pauses to suck down some more beer. "I'm taking her out to dinner this weekend."

"Ohh la la. She can roll her eyes at you by candlelight."

"Hey, there's been a 50-percent decrease in eye-rolling. And I don't think there's candlelight. It's not a fancy place—that's not her jam. It's sort of low-key and artsy."

"No wonder she and Spence are friends. They sound crazy similar."

"Oh, they definitely are, from what I can tell." He nudges me. "Have you taken Spencer out or anything since disc golf?"

"Uhhh." I'm not sure how I'd explain all the things Spencer and I have done, though I'm pretty sure library hanging, window masturbation, and sneaky blowjobs don't qualify as dates. "Not really."

"So start there if you're into him."

"I think I might." I crack up at his smug expression. "Don't sit there acting like you're Mr. Romance when you're equally clueless." Mr. Romance is well-known on campus for coming up with awesome dates for the inept. I don't think I'm inept, though. I just haven't been properly motivated in a long time.

Now I am.

Tommy, Royer's friend from Stormer house—aka Stoner house—drops into an open chair next to Royer, reeking of weed and effectively ending our dating discussion.

While Royer launches into an animated explanation of DIKcon, I keep an eye on Spencer, considering how to ask him out for a real date as I watch him zip among tables and patrons. He stops briefly at the bar, cracking up at something the surly bartender, Brax, says. I'm only half-aware of the goofy smile painting my face until Royer slugs me in the arm.

"Hey, Cheeseball, did you hear what I said?"

My gaze lingers another beat on Spencer before I reluctantly drag it away and tune in to the conversation. "Something about Stormer house and DIKcon?"

"Yeah, Tommy thinks he can recruit the whole house."

"Badass. The more, the merrier. Everyone's invited."

"I make no promises about Chris, though." Tommy huffs a strand of hair from his forehead and chuckles. "He's got himself all wrapped up in this science major, Aiden, that he's been crushing on since freshman year."

I don't know Chris as more than a passing acquaintance, but Royer perks with interest. "Damn, I know a little bit about unrequited crushes. There's this girl…" he says, and they're off again.

Royer ditches a half hour later to get high with Tommy, and I'm on my way out, too, but I linger near one of the server stations to see if I can grab Spencer for a second. I flash a peace sign at Ty, one of FU's lacrosse players, as he passes with a bin of dirty dishes on his way to the kitchen. According to Spencer, the dude hates other people's dirty dishes.

"Gonna clean those with your tongue?" I tease, and crack up when he mimics retching. He then flips me the bird before passing through the doorway.

Spencer drops off another tray and finally heads in my direction, a tiny smile curving his lips. "How drunk are you?"

"Not very. Maybe medium drunk." Makes sense to me.

"What does medium drunk entail?"

"Two more glasses of water before bed and I'm good to go in the morning."

"I'm a lightweight." Spencer fiddles with the string on his apron and leans against the wall. "But apparently highly entertaining."

"I don't doubt that." The idea of a drunk Spencer makes me smile. I tug on the apron string he's fiddling with. "I'm taking you out somewhere Thursday afternoon to celebrate getting that interview." I know for sure he doesn't have a shift at Shenanigans that night because it's usually when he shows up at the library.

"Where?" Spencer looks left, then right, then back at me. "Is there an alternate Spencer you already coordinated this with, considering there was no question mark involved just now?"

Right. Technically you're supposed to ask for a date, but with Spencer, I figure it's best to just throw it out there and see if it sticks. "C'mon, it'll be fun."

He gives me a dubious squint of his eyes. "Where are we going?"

"Surprise. Don't ruin it, just go with it."

I totally expect him to protest and demand to know where I'm taking him, but after a beat, a smile twitches at the corners of his mouth, and he says, "Okay."

That was easier than anticipated.

17

SPENCER

Cory's whole demeanor shifts the second we step foot on the wooden planks of the dock. He always carries himself confidently, but there's an added lightness to his steps that wasn't there before. His shoulders are looser. I don't want to notice it because it makes me feel *things*, but somehow, I can't help it. He stops in front of a white catamaran with script lettering reading *Gaia* and turns to me. "We're going sailing."

"For real?" I want to protest on sheer principle, but I can't find a spare principle. The boat is gorgeous. Sleek, shiny, and obviously well cared for. Cory's affable grin as he nods is equally bright. The weather is perfect, and damn, I've always wanted to go sailing on a boat like this. "This your uncle's?"

"Yep, and you're overdue for your maiden voyage." He hops onto the boat and extends a hand. "C'mon. I'll need your help."

"Wait, you do know how to drive this thing, right?"

Cory slaps his forehead. "Shit, I knew I forgot something. Maybe we can make it go with paddles?"

"Smart-ass," I say, his hand warm over mine as I step carefully into the boat, worried I might knock something expensive loose.

"So I've been upgraded from dumbass to smart-ass now?" Cory regards me with amusement. "You really do like me."

"Don't get cocky." I tug my hand out of his and instead help him with the ropes.

"Why not? I happen to really like when you get cocky. Can't it go both ways?" He arches a brow suggestively, and I turn away with a grin and a shake of my head.

"It always comes back to my dick."

"Entire civilizations have risen and fallen around dicks. And you happen to have one I really like." He glances over again. "The rest of you is pretty great, too."

"Flattery isn't required to see my dick again. I'm happy to show you anytime." I side-eye him, but he seems genuine.

"Maybe we should get out of the marina first." Cory winks and then moves to the boat's wheel, cranking it up.

I stroll the deck, taking in the boat. There are seats and a big backrest, a control panel with a bunch of dials, levers, buttons, and screens that are incomprehensible to me. When I look at Cory, he's already busy and seems to know what he's doing. "You can really sail this thing?"

"Promise. I'll give you a tour once we get going." He tips his head toward a yellow cooler nearby. "Open that up."

When I do, I find an assortment of food, soda, water, and beer. "Is that a charcuterie? How did this even get here?" Lifestyles of the rich and the famous are clearly beyond me.

"There's a service that puts together picnic baskets and stuff," he says, because of course there is, and of course Cory knows all about it.

I'm ridiculously out of my element, but I try to play it cool. A charcuterie, though? Seriously? I have to fight a smile. It's kind of endearing.

"So where are we going?"

"Just far enough out to see the coastline once it gets dark. It's gorgeous." He twists a dial. "Unless you've got other plans later, of course."

My heart stutters. Is this an actual date? It's starting to feel like one, and the problem is I'm enjoying it. "No plans," I murmur, distracted as he bends over and pulls out a couple of life jackets that he sets on one of the benches. Damn his perfect ass.

"Awesome." He grins when he catches me looking at him. "Go sit up on the front. That's the best view."

I make my way to the front of the catamaran and plop down, glancing back and studying Cory as he fiddles with levers and gauges. God, he's gorgeous, and despite my intent not to let myself get caught up in him, I am. I like being with him. I like that he's not put off by my grumpiness. I like that he thinks I'm sexy. His mere presence has become a full-frontal assault on my emotions and my dick, and I'm not sure I care to stop it anymore.

When the boat lurches forward, I startle and promptly hear Cory's laughter from behind me. I flip him a bird, but I'm smiling. Cory puts a hand on the wheel, face drawn with concentration, losing himself in the task at hand. Unlike me, he's very much in his element. No wonder he loved the charter fishing gig. It seems perfectly him, and I frown at the idea of him tucked in some high-rise office in NYC coming up with ad campaigns for the latest product.

We're quickly out of the marina and onto the water. I watch the coastline, the sun beating down on it, the water reflecting the sky. I don't remember it ever being this blue.

Something about the way the air smells and the way the late-afternoon sun dances on the water sends a rare rush of contentment through me. I spend so much time on the go between classes and my job that I rarely ever sit down and enjoy the world I'm studying. I get so caught up in trying to learn the material, trying to ace an assignment, or trying to impress the profs for that ever-elusive A or a dazzling paper that I don't really think about what I'm doing. Or what I might be missing out on. I'm also acutely aware of Cory and the way he's looking at me, his gaze hot and intense, as if I'm the only thing he can see.

I can't think of anywhere I'd rather be right now.

Once we're well away from the marina, Cory joins me. I shoot an alarmed look over my shoulder at the abandoned helm.

"Settle down. We're not going fast, and I've got autopilot engaged." He tweaks a lock of hair whipping against the side of my face.

"You sure?"

"Pretty sure. I mean, I've only done this a couple hundred times in my life."

"Okay." I relax as he sits down next to me, his shoulder touching mine. The simple point of contact is comforting. "It's nice just to sit here and let the world go by for a change."

"You don't get a lot of downtime." It's a statement, not a question.

"Nope." I want to apologize for all my grouchiness and be the kind of guy he thinks I am. But all I can really offer him is the truth. "I should try to get more, but..."

Cory holds my gaze for a long moment, searching me in his usual Cory way. It makes me nervous, but I don't look away because this time, I don't mind him reading whatever is there.

After a few beats, his mouth curves, and before I fully register what's happening, our lips meet gently. The kiss tastes of sea salt and fresh air and doesn't last nearly long enough, but god does it leave me weak.

"Why are you smiling?" Cory asks when we part for a breath,

eyes dancing with self-aware humor. "I thought that was a thing you didn't do with me."

I swat him lightly. "I'm not sure. It's just... everything. Little things." I glance around with a laugh. "Or big things, like this catamaran that probably costs more than my life."

"Maybe like half your life. But I get what you're saying." He brushes a strand of hair from his eyes. "I'd feel this way even on a little outboard. It's the water and the sun for me." His gaze goes thoughtful for a moment, and then he smacks a palm against his thigh and stands, offering me his hand. "Want to try sailing?"

"Uhhhh, do I?" Putting me in charge of hundreds of thousands of dollars' worth of machinery? That sounds like a bad idea, but Cory seems amused by my skepticism as he pulls me upright.

"Yup. I'll give you a crash course, and you can take it from there." He places his hands on my hips, his thumbs grazing the bare skin at my waist and sending a shiver through me. I want more of him, definitely. I want us naked and tangled up in each other.

TURNS OUT SAILING ISN'T SO DIFFICULT. AT LEAST NOT WHEN YOU have an experienced guide, all the latest gadgets and thingamabobs, and plenty of open water. Okay, so it's nerve-racking as shit, but Cory is next to me the entire time, pointing out various instruments, the sails, using a ton of terms that immediately flit from my memory because, let's be honest, he's distracting. His smile is distracting, and his clear enjoyment of being out on the ocean is infectious.

We run the catamaran back and forth parallel to the shore

and finally drop anchor when the sun begins to sink toward the horizon.

Cory gives me a tour of the boat's luxurious interior with a king-size bed in the master cabin that both of us stand there considering.

I know what I'm thinking, and I'm pretty sure I know what Cory's thinking, too. When our eyes meet, my cheeks heat, and Cory grins, waggling his brows. "Maybe do a quality check on this later?"

"Later?" I question because now seems like a good time. For all of our various activities together, we've never been in an actual bed. Part of that, at least at first, was me and my stubbornness. But now I'd really like to know how it would feel being horizontal with him.

"Later, yeah." He tugs my hand. "I want you to see the sunset."

We return to the front of the boat with the food and drinks Cory has brought with him, snacking and talking as we watch the sun drop toward the water.

It's a gorgeous orange and pink sunset over the ocean, its colors reflected in the gentle swells that are almost hypnotizing. We're especially quiet as we watch it, but when it's finally gone and the night sky has taken over, Cory turns to me.

"I like that smile on you." He brushes a finger along said curve.

"I like all of your smiles," I admit and earn a flash of his dimple in return. "Though if I have to rank them, the smug one comes in last."

Cory scoffs. "I have no such smile. You're making that up."

"You totally do. It was all I used to see when we first started..." I don't know what to call it. Hanging out? We're definitely hanging out now, but before, I guess we were just hooking up. Given my inexperience with relationships, I'm not even sure how to categorize it. But what's scarier is that in the moment, I don't care. I just know it's something. "When you first started badgering me," I tease. There, that works well enough.

He leans closer, his lips a featherlight caress over mine. "And what about this? Does this qualify as badgering?"

"No, this qualifies as temptation." And a whole hell of a lot of it. I think about that bed below deck, and once again, Cory seems on the same track.

"Let's go inside?" It's a question, but his voice is a low, rumbling purr I can't resist. I twine my fingers through his.

We clean up our mess on the deck and move inside.

The second we're in the cabin, his lips touch my neck, and his hands are on my hips, moving me forward. I turn around, and he cups my jaw, mouth finding mine. He kisses me deeply, and I sigh, sinking into him, wrapping my arms around his neck and kissing him back with equal fervor. The boat rocks gently from side to side, and with our bodies touching, I can feel that rocking all over. The sensation is incredible, coupled with the feeling of Cory's mouth on me, his hands on me. God, I want him, I want this.

I want to push him down on the bed and climb on top of him and never come up for air.

Cory's hands settle on my ass, his grip tightening as we move against each other with too much clothing between us.

His shirt comes off, then mine. I map his chest with my mouth and hands, lingering over every curve and dip as his hands move over my back.

"We've, ummm... I don't think we've ever discussed preferences specifically," I say when we break for air, and his mouth hooks up.

"I don't think we have. So what're yours?" His gaze drops to my erection, a hungry gleam in his eyes.

"Vers. It's been a while since I've bottomed. But it's been

a while since I've topped, too. It's been a while since anything," I confess. It's a little embarrassing. My last hookup before Cory, we traded blowjobs. The time before that, I can't even remember, but I think I topped. Before I hung out more with Cory, I'd have totally pegged him as a top.

He's got a toppy vibe, but neither am I surprised when he says, "I like it all. Sometimes I'm in the mood for one thing, sometimes another. But right now..." His gaze dips to my dick again, and he inhales softly. "I'll fuck you any way you want me to. On your knees or on top... anything you want, but I think what I'd really love is to feel your cock inside me. I've been thinking about it for days. Weeks."

Weeks? My pulse hammers at my temples, my heart on fire. A needy groan slips past my throat in response, and my cock twitches in anticipation of pushing inside him. "Condoms... lube," I murmur as I yank him closer, already so wound up that words are hard.

Cory's expression is slightly sheepish as he flings an arm aside and pulls open a drawer on the table next to the bed. Inside is a fresh box of condoms and tube of lube.

"Not sure how I feel about using your uncle's stuff," I tease. "Or you're just overly confident."

"Optimistic and hopeful, not necessarily confident. And you know damn well those aren't my uncle's."

I reach for the lube and condoms, then for him. He's already shoved his pants down, and I take the opportunity to kiss his cock, licking from base to tip, then sucking the head into my mouth and swirling my tongue around it.

"Goddamn, yeah," he mutters, hands fisting my hair and tugging gently.

I revel in the feeling of his cock in my mouth, the power I have over him, then sit up and kiss him deeply. While he's distracted, I flip him onto the bed, pulling his pants all the way off and grinding myself hard against his ass.

"God, I love your cock," Cory moans, and I nearly come all over his ass at that second. I don't feel self-conscious or awkward around him; I feel fucking sexy, which, believe me, is not a feeling I experience a lot.

"Will you ride me?" I ask. That'll give him more control with the depth. I roll my hips against his tight ass again and shudder at the way my cock glides along his crease. Cory gives a soft moan in response, then a louder "Fuck yeah."

I flop onto my back, my hard dick rebounding against my stomach. Cory straddles my thighs and reaches down, stroking himself at the same time he strokes me.

"Not gonna lie, I think you're the biggest I've ever had."

"That was kinda my intro to bottoming. The first guy I ever fooled around with in high school took one look at my dick and said no way."

Cory chuckles. "Yeah, well, I like a challenge." His expression darkens briefly, and then he leans over and kisses me. I hear the cap of the lube snap open, and he reaches behind himself, smearing it over his hole before he grabs my hand and guides it lower. "A little help?"

I urge him higher on my chest so his cock is close enough for me to engulf, sucking on the head, swirling my tongue around the slit. Then I work him with my hand, taking the time to map his length and the sensation of his silky skin against my palm. His cock is thick and perfect, and I don't want to take my mouth off him, but I want to see him take me.

I groan softly and run my fingers over his ass, smearing the lube, teasing his hole, then slipping a couple of fingers inside. He arches into the sensation, legs spread wide to give me room, and I play with his hole while he works his cock in my fist, then lean up and kiss him.

Cory bucks his hips, driving himself back against my fingers. I slip in a third, and his hand drops from mine. He reaches back, his ass muscles clenching around the invasion as he spreads lube over my cock. "Jesus, fuck yes," he murmurs, as I glide my fingers in and out, curling them to rub over his prostate. "Just like that."

He nudges my wrist, and I ease my fingers free as he rises higher on his knees and guides my cock to his entrance. I let out a steadying exhale as he rubs the head over his hole slowly, back and forth, until we're both panting and ready for more. It takes a second for me to register the increase in heat, the slow, tight give of his body as he takes me inside, just the tip.

"Shit," he whispers.

"Okay?" I check and pray he says yes, because he already feels so damn good I can't even imagine what it'll be like when I'm fully inside him.

"Fuck yes," he rasps.

We both groan when my cock slides deeper, disappearing into his body as his ass clenches around me. He pauses, adjusting, then slowly lowers down again on a long exhale. I watch as he rocks up and down, his cheekbones flushed, nipples hard. He's beautiful, muscular, thick, glistening with sweat, eyes bright, his mouth parted. I can't take my eyes off the sight of him riding me. The visuals are going to be burned into my brain forever.

I reach up and wrap my hand around his flushed cock, tugging gently. His eyes flutter closed, then open, dazed.

"You feel amazing," I manage when I can gulp for air. "So fucking tight."

"Fuck, Spencer." He rocks his hips, moving faster. He's close; with each stroke, his face tightens, his expression twists into a grimace, and his hands grip the sheets on either side of my head.

I fist my hands in his hair like I'm hanging on for dear life and trying not to lose it before he does.

"I'm gonna come," Cory groans.

Pulling him closer, I thrust up into him, holding his hips in place, extending his pleasure. He clenches around me, and his head drops back, muscles straining. I kiss the exposed skin of his neck. My cock feels like it's on fire inside him, and I'm desperate for him to break, for him to come so I can lose myself inside him.

My orgasm creeps up on me, my cock thickening impossibly, pushing my limits. Balls tightening, my movements grow more erratic. I'm dimly aware of Cory bucking his hips, his hard cock rubbing against me in a frenzy, his body tensing like a coiled spring.

A flash of white light explodes behind my eyelids, a burst of heat and pleasure, and then I'm lost in ecstasy. My cock throbs in the tight grip of his ass, and I can feel his body spasm with his own orgasm.

"Shit," he gasps, the roll of his hips relentless as he rides me through it. He keeps going until I'm damn near numb and noodle-armed, then collapses against me, his heart thumping against my chest.

"Wow," he whispers, and I echo him. My body is spent and I don't even bother to move. I feel completely relaxed, completely content, completely sated in every way. I've never experienced anything like this, not even close.

"I hate to admit it, but your rep for sexual prowess isn't unearned." Though I get a little flash of jealousy thinking about it, which I know is dumb. I was watching him long before we were anything, which also begs the question as we lie here in each other's arms: What are we now?

Cory exhales a drowsy laugh. "I hardly did anything. You're

the one wielding the power tool. God, I don't think I've ever had a p-spot buzz like that."

"Stop," I say but can't deny the thrill in my chest. Cory Ingram thinks I'm a good lay. Hell, Cory Ingram might actually be into me, and I'm very definitely into him. A lot more than I've allowed myself to feel.

We lie there for a while, legs tangled, trying to remember how our bodies function.

"I guess we should head back soon," I say reluctantly. I don't want to leave this night behind, but I do need to be fresh for my interview tomorrow.

Cory rolls toward me, a smile playing over his lips. "Your interview isn't until ten. What if we stay out here tonight and I swear I'll have you back with time to spare?"

I hedge, but I'm powerless against the lazy mirth in his molten eyes, the sensation of his warm, firm body against mine, and just for one night, it'd be nice to be carefree. I trust him. "If we stay, can we go again?"

"Already? Jesus, man, are you harboring secret superpowers? Are you not actually cosplaying at all?"

"You never know." I grin and wiggle my fingers at him. "You top this time."

He rolls over on top of me comically fast, crushing my lips against his. "Oh, it's on now."

18

CORY

"Wake up!" The frantic hissing and the jostling of my shoulder makes me crack an eye. Spencer's face is right there, and damn he looks good in the morning.

Except for that panicked expression.

"What time is it?" I ask blearily. Surely there's enough time to snuggle, maybe even get another round in. My watch alarm hasn't even gone off yet.

"It's eight! My interview is at ten." He begins tossing clothes at me as I bolt upright. "I thought you set an alarm."

"I did," I insist. "I thought you did, too."

"One of us must have turned it off." His accusing stare suggests it was me, and when I glance at the nightstand next to me where our phones are, I decide that's probably the case. Shit. I check my phone alarm, too.

Double shit. "Fuck, my dumb ass set it for 6:00 p.m. instead of a.m."

"Jesus!" Spencer throws his hands up.

"Cumdrunk, I guess. Sorry." An unfamiliar sheepish edge creeps into my voice, but Spencer's lips do soften into a brief smile before he yanks the covers off me.

"We need to go, like, now."

I stretch and nod. "Settle down, it's fine. We're, like, a half hour from shore. Plenty of time."

"I wanted to go over my questions again. And I need to shower and…"

I yank Spencer down and silence him with my mouth, pleased when he melts into the kiss. At least for a second. Last night is still wrapped around me like a warm fog, and I'm reluctant to leave. I want to do it all again, like immediately, but I detach after a few seconds. "You're going to have plenty of time. Promise. We'll go right now."

"Okay." Some of the anxiety in his tone ebbs as I climb from the bed.

"I'll have us going in under five minutes." I bang my head on the cabin's threshold as I stumble toward the back of the boat, but the sharp pain is a good wake-up call.

I blink in the sunlight long enough for my eyes to adjust, then race to pull up the anchor before heading starboard to crank the catamaran. The rumble of a boat engine coming to life is a nostalgic, soothing sound to me.

And one that's decidedly lacking this morning.

I frown down at the helm. Did I do something wrong? I check the instrument panel and then attempt to start the engine again. Nothing.

Spencer pokes his head out from below deck. "You said under five minutes. It's been 5:45."

"Yeah, I'm on it. It's, uhhh…" I check the dials for the third time, and try once more.

The color drains from Spencer's face. "You're fucking kidding me. Please tell me you're kidding me."

"I've got it. I'll figure it out. Just give me a second."

"I don't have a second. I… fuck." Spencer puts his face in his hands and inhales deeply. "I knew this was a bad idea. The worst idea."

I step away from the wheel and circle his wrists gently, pulling them free of his face. "I will get you there on time, I promise you, okay? Just give me a couple of minutes, and try not to freak out?"

He nods, but his pinched expression says he's already freaking out anyway. And to be honest, I am, too. This interview is basically the most important thing to Spencer ever, and if I fuck this up for him, I'll feel goddamn awful. Guilt and anxiety roil in my gut as I try to work through everything I know about catamarans and why the engines might possibly not start. Panic isn't going to help, so I pace the deck and take a few deep breaths to clear my mind. The battery shouldn't be dead. I know that. I run through my memory of other instances when this has occurred, because it's happened before, and then I have my starting points.

I return to the controls, make sure the safety features were off—check—that I didn't make an error in the starting sequence —check. So that leaves me to go under the hood, so to speak. I check the battery connection, then the air vents and exhaust, all good. Plenty of gas. I study the fuel lines and... "I've got it," I shout. The line is kinked, no clue how. But once I get that sorted, I hop back up on deck, and the boat roars to life.

"We're good!" I tell Spencer, beaming with triumph, but his expression is still miserable, and I get why when I glance at the clock on my phone again.

"It's fine," he mumbles. "I'm just going to miss it. I'll see if I can come up with a good excuse or something. Maybe they'll let me reschedule."

"You're not going to miss it," I vow.

I turn the boat around and set off at the fastest clip I can manage. With the engine at full throttle, the wind roars past us, and the sun and sea are a kaleidoscope of brilliant, hypnotic shades of blue, but my adrenaline is entirely focused on getting Spencer there on time, on giving him the opportunity to show the interview committee what he's made of. As we approach the shoreline, I keep the engine at full speed until the last possible moment before it causes a safety issue getting into the marina. "Almost there," I holler at Spencer, but when I glance aside, he's not there. I know he didn't jump overboard to swim the rest of the way to shore, but this interview is so important to him I might not have been surprised.

And I still feel awful for cutting it so close.

Spencer reappears from below deck moments later as I guide the boat into its slip, freshly shaven, his hair combed neatly. "I found a razor in the bathroom. Hope it's okay that I used it."

"Of course. I'm really sorry," I apologize again, speaking hastily as I hop onto the dock, dragging a line after me to secure to the nearest cleat. "That totally wasn't what I intended to happen." And I definitely didn't intend to be so... mind-blown over our night together. "Spence. Spencer," I correct. "I had a really good time last night." I extend my hand for him. "C'mon, go. You've got this."

"It was..." Spencer takes my hand and hops onto the dock next to me, lingering even as I urge him forward. He glances at his phone, then shakes his head. "Shit, I don't have time for this. Thanks for the boat ride, though. That was cool. And last night, and..." He waves a hand. "Right, no time."

I bite back a grin, calling after his hastily retreating form. "Let me know how it goes. I know you're gonna kill it."

As soon as he vanishes, I plop down right there on the dock, waiting for my heart to quit racing. That was way too close for comfort.

Once I've settled down, I change the bed linens, get the boat cleaned up, and head back to the frat house.

"Ohh la la. Is Ingram doing the walk of shame?" Javi teases as I come in the back door. I mean, it's pretty obvious since I'm wearing my clothes from the day before. Now's the time I'd usually brag about getting laid or at least acknowledge it. But... I just can't do it. The words won't come, and what's more, I don't even want to tell anyone about my night with Spencer because it was that fucking good. I haven't seriously been into anyone in years, but I'm very definitely into him, and I'm weirdly protective of whatever is going on between us.

So I shake my head with a laugh. "Nah, my dumb ass just took out the catamaran and passed out."

"Goddamn, Ingram. Well, how about next time you invite us along? That boat is sweet."

"Next time, yeah. I promise," I say, then head upstairs to shower and get ready for my class, keeping an eye on my phone for any message from Spencer.

But nothing comes.

19

CORY

I've not heard from Spencer since this morning, when I sent him a text right before his interview apologizing again for the boat mishap and wishing him good luck. He sent me back a thanks with a smiley face and then... nothing.

I know he had a shift at Shenanigans in the early afternoon, and I know he's alive because when I asked a couple of guys who'd gone to Shenanigans for a late lunch, they said he was there working and then proceeded to rib me about it. It makes sense, considering I rarely show extended interest in someone, much less ask about them. And after last night, Spencer is heavily on my mind because... fuck, I can't stop thinking about him.

I finally send him another text when I know for sure he should be done with his shift.

Cory: *You're keeping me in suspense, dude. How'd it go?*

I should probably be embarrassed by how much my heart leaps when I see he's replying.

Spencer: *I bombed it.*
Cory: *Not possible.*
Spencer: *No, I really did. I got flustered, stuttered like an idiot through the whole thing, and I know for sure I came off as unprepared.*
Cory: *I think you're overthinking it, but I get that. I know it's important to you. Want to hang out, have a beer, and chill? I'll even give you a back rub.*
Spencer: *Darby is forcing me to go to a cosplay meet-up to drown my sorrows.*

I frown, though I guess I shouldn't be surprised that I wasn't invited. Spencer doesn't owe me anything, and maybe he just wants to hang out with Darby solo. Still, it stings a little.

Cory: *Okay, I hope you have fun. There's a kegger at DIK house later. You and Darby are welcome to come to it if you want.*

I hesitate, typing out, "I'd love to see you," before erasing it.

THREE HOURS LATER, I REFILL MY BEER FROM ONE OF THE COPIOUS kegs scattered throughout the DIK house and lawn. Another Friday night, another party. Try as I might, I'm having trouble getting into it. Spencer is the only thing on my mind. He thumbs-upped my last text without further reply, and now I totally get Royer's hatred for the thumbs-up. It's irritatingly vague.

Royer nudges me, chin tipping toward a collection of guys and girls at the pool table. "Sarah was talking about how hot you are earlier. I overheard it." He waggles his brows as I pick Sarah out from the crowd. Hot brunette, killer smile that she aims in my direction with a wink when she catches me looking, though I offer only a polite smile in return.

Sarah was definitely on my hit list once, but I'm not even sure my hit list exists anymore, and it's tripping me up. "Meh," I say unenthusiastically and gulp some more beer, because beer is excellent medicine for insecurity, right? It's barely going on midnight, and I'm already considering bed. Tomorrow, I'm gonna seek Spencer out in person and tell him that I want more with him.

Turns out I don't have to wait until tomorrow.

A hubbub rises from the hallway, and then Jackson bursts into the common area, where I've migrated, hooting, "There's a hammered Spider-Man here. Should I see him out or..."

I've got a pretty good idea of who's behind the mask, so I step around Royer. "Where is he? I'll take care of it."

Jackson gestures behind him, and I make my way through revelers until I spot him.

Spencer is at one of the kegs, fiddling with the tap and failing. He doesn't have a mask on, his usually tidy locks in disarray, but the Spider-Man costume hugs his lean form like a fucking glove. My eyes move over him, and I have to urge them to keep going up when they dally over the prominent bulge in the front, and I remember with a delicious twinge of heat how it felt to ride him last night, his hands on my thighs, the wanton thrusts. In any other situation, my mouth would be watering, but he's also, judging by his lack of coordination with the tap, completely blitzed.

Another girl is dipping down to help him when I slip behind them and grab the tap from Spencer's hand. "I think you're good, Spence."

"You." His gaze swings toward me, the hazy cast of his eyes sharpening. "Don't call me Spence."

"No take-backs. I've called you that multiple times lately, and you don't say shit. I earned Spence rights."

"I hereby revoke them." He waves a hand and wobbles.

"Nope. I won't allow it." I grab his bicep to steady him. "I take it the thing with Darby was a good time?"

"Maybe it was? I don't know." He wrinkles his nose. "No, wait. I'm getting distracted again. That's the problem with you. You're distracting."

"Sounds more like a compliment," I say, but my smile fades when he doesn't return it.

He shakes his head vehemently. "I need to have a word with you… right after I refill this beer. I need another beer."

"How about we have a word over some water?" I suggest, reaching down to grab one from a cooler nearby. Yes, we stock water at our parties. DIKs aren't total dicks, and dehydration sucks.

"No, I think beer is better." Spencer eyes the water dubiously. "Actually, I think I need a restroom first."

That I can help with. I put a hand on his shoulder and guide him into the hallway, bypassing the downstairs bathrooms and urging him up the stairs, which he trips over twice. I catch him by an elbow the second time, and he shakes off my touch with an indignant "I've got it."

On the second floor, I lead him down the hallway toward my room, where there's a shared bathroom that's much quieter, less active, and a whole helluva lot cleaner than the ones downstairs.

"Don't go anywhere." He narrows his eyes as I hold the door open for him.

"I can promise you I'm not gonna move an inch."

His breath catches, and then he fully scowls and disappears into a stall. I haven't missed that scowl at all.

"You're a bad distraction, Cory Ingram, and I can't have

distractions right now. Can't afford them," he says as he takes a whiz.

I bark out a laugh. The pit of my stomach told me something was off between us, but distracting? I can totally handle that. Way better than Spencer just outright saying he doesn't like me or want to see me anymore. "You're gonna come at me for being 'distracting' mid-pee while dressed as Spider-Man?" This is highly amusing. Then again, he did tell me he was entertaining while drunk.

Silence, and then he exits the stall. My amusement fades. His expression is drawn and defeated. "I really did fuck up my interview today. I was distracted, couldn't calm down, couldn't stop thinking about last night, and I sounded like a babbling idiot."

I lean against the wall beside him. "I'm sure it wasn't that bad. You're articulate and smart and..."

"No, trust me." He shakes his head woefully. "It was bad. If I could have recorded it and shown it to you, you would've cringed with secondhand embarrassment."

I want to tell him that I wouldn't, that I think he's smart and capable, sexy and funny, and the panel he spoke in front of surely saw that, too. Except for the sexy part, because that would just be weird.

But I open my mouth at the same time he goes pale and claps a hand over his, lurching for the bathroom.

"Shit," I mutter as he hurls in the toilet. "Don't move."

"Can't," he gasps, so I race to my room, coming back with a washcloth that I wet in the sink before nudging the stall door open and crouching behind him.

"Damn, what the hell have you been drinking?" I lay the cloth over the back of his neck. "Looks like a unicorn hurled in this toilet."

"I don't know. Some pink fruity things. Watermelon mojitos.

Maybe some bellinis. Tasted good at the time. Second round, I give zero out of ten."

"Sorry," I whisper as he's racked again. "Shouldn't have said that."

He groans, and I hop up to rewet the cloth, this time swiping over his forehead and mouth.

His eyes fall shut. "God, that feels good."

I keep wiping him down until he seems to have emptied his stomach and rests his head against the side of the stall with a mumbled "This feels nice, too."

"Nooooo." I reach out and hook his elbow as his eyes flutter shut. I'm not about to let him fall asleep in a frat house bathroom. Talk about regrets.

He lets me guide him up, and we shuffle awkwardly to my bedroom, where he blinks rapidly. "I can't stay here."

"It's fine. Just rest for a few minutes, okay? No one will bother you in here."

"Stop being nice."

Another laugh escapes me as I throw up my hands. "I can't win with you."

He drops into my desk chair and starts kicking at his boots. I kneel in front of him to help. "This costume is pretty fucking impressive, I've gotta admit," I tell him as I peel one of the boots off.

"Thanks." He lets out another miserable groan and sags in the chair. "Darby took me to a cosplay meetup at Bar Lucerne to try and cheer me up."

"Yes, you mentioned that a time or five already. Looks like that went great." I yank the other boot off and toss it aside as Spencer bats at me and misses.

"It's really fucking annoying how nice you're being right now while I'm trying to be irritated at you."

"Well, that's a new one. Judged for being too nice." Wait. I glance up at him. "You're *trying* to be irritated with me?"

"Mm-hmm. Because you're distracting. And attractive. You're super fucking attractive. And a great kisser and... great at lots of other things, and I totally lied when I said I didn't like you. Even the first time. I just didn't *want* to like you, because so many people do and... why bother? It's not like you ever keep anyone around anyway or like I'd know how to keep you."

The last words hit me square in the chest, a pang radiating outward. There's a reason for that, but all of them seem sort of flimsy now. I've been on such a mission to be the life of the party, to have fun, that I've not really left myself time for anyone to get in, to go deeper. And while I'll never believe there's anything wrong with having lots of sexual experiences, I can admit that maybe I've shortchanged myself on having something more meaningful and long-lasting. I didn't want that before, and now....?

I gaze up at Spencer, and even in his sloppy, hair askew, piqued state, I get a funny feeling in my stomach. A warmth, a sense of possessiveness mixed with desire.

"Why are you looking at me like that?" he demands.

"Because I think you're really fucking..." God, now is definitely not the time to tell him how deep my feelings are for him, especially when I'm being berated for being nice. I'm not sure how well it would go over. I have serious doubts he's going to remember any of this anyway, and I really want him to. "Cute. You're really cute, and you need to get your ass in this bed and get some sleep."

"I can't." He shakes his head. "I'll just walk back to the house."

"Spence, just get in the damn bed. Nothing's gonna happen except sleep."

He starts to rise, then flops back into the chair, face paling again. "Okay, attempting to walk was a bad idea."

"You need to never drink a—"

He whips his hand around. "Don't even say the word out loud unless you want me to hurl again."

"Done. Now, lemme help you." I sling an arm around him and guide him to my bed. "You look really fucking hot as Spider-Man, by the way."

"I know." He sighs. "It's not quite Tom Holland doing Rihanna's 'Umbrella,' but still hot."

"Hmmm?" I'm half-distracted, trying to peel off the gloves he's wearing.

"Google it. One of the best moments in the history of TV, I swear." He exhales a gusty sigh. "I watch it whenever I need a pick-me-up. Probably watched it ten times today. I shouldn't tell you that. Sounds kinda pathetic."

I make a mental note to check it out, then get the gloves off and toss them aside as he flops back on the bed.

"How about I help you out of the rest of this costume?" No way that much spandex is comfortable to sleep in.

"Are we going to fuck again?"

I chuckle. "Definitely not when you're in this state."

"Oh, bummer. I really enjoyed that. I mean, minus the part where I woke up in a panic and then the part where I totally bombed my interview."

I still can't imagine he bombed the interview, but I don't argue with him. It's his other comment that catches me off guard. "So you really enjoyed last night? Or just the fucking?"

"Both." He sighs again. "Except for the part where I woke up in a panic and then the part where—"

"You think you bombed your interview, yeah, you just said that."

"Oh, well, it's still true."

"So, about this costume. I can get you some boxers and a tee?"

He waves a hand faintly. "Nah, I'm good just like this."

I eye the Spider-Man in my bed skeptically, but his eyelids are heavy, and he does look close to passing out. I don't want to risk upsetting his stomach again by forcing him to change, so after grabbing a couple of waters from my minifridge and setting them on the table beside him, I shuck my clothes and crawl in bed next to him. He immediately snuggles up as close as he can, his body molding around me.

"Feels good," he murmurs.

It does. The feeling of Spencer against me again, of his breath on my neck, of his whole body against mine, is perfect. I pick up my phone in one hand, the other wrapped around him. Then, turning the volume on low, I find the clip that he's talking about. I watch it straight through, twice with a growing smile. Tom comes onstage dancing and lip-synching to "Singin' in the Rain," then rips off his suit to reveal a French maid costume underneath and proceeds to rock the hell out of "Umbrella" in a pair of heels. It's sexy and clever as fuck. Spencer would look equally hot in a French maid costume. I grin as I ponder whether I might be able to convince him to do a cosplay like that sometime. Would it even count? Can you cosplay actors?

As I drift off, it occurs to me that Spencer Crowe is the first person I've ever had stay overnight since I came to FU.

20

SPENCER

I'm surrounded by the warmth of Cory's body, the weight of him on top of me, the firm lines of his muscles under my hands where I'm gripping his biceps as he thrusts into me. I was frustrated with him, but I forget now for what, and it doesn't matter. All that matters is thrust after thrust, each movement sending cascades of pleasure through my body. His lips brush over mine, his voice soft as he reaches between us and grabs my aching cock. My climax overtakes me, and I writhe as I erupt.

I blink my eyes open.

Above me is ceiling that's not mine. I turn a bleary-eyed gaze on the warm lump next to me.

Cory. Cory?

Confusion pings off the still-fuzzy corners of my mind, and I note faintly that my crotch is cool and wet.

Carefully, I peer below the sheets and stifle a gasp, horror racing through me as I realize what's happened.

Who the hell has a wet dream while sleeping in someone else's bed? And while wearing a Spider-Man costume, no less. Holy heck.

My whole body flames with embarrassment. What am I, thirteen?

Cory mumbles something that sounds like "where are you going?" and reaches out an arm.

"Bathroom," I mutter and roll upright. All I can think of is cleaning up. God, I do not want Cory to know I just splooged in his bed after a dream. Quietly, I grab up the rest of my costume from the floor. I don't have my phone and have no idea what time it is, but my guess is early morning, and hopefully, after last night's DIK party, which I vaguely remember now, everyone will still be asleep. Probably best for me to just head out. I can touch base with Cory later and apologize for being a drunken idiot. I'm not sure what all I said, but the fact that he's in bed next to me is promising. I hope.

Shame still burning the back of my neck, I peek into the bathroom. It's thankfully empty, and a quick assessment in the mirror shows the wet spot on the front of my costume isn't too noticeable. I briefly consider going back into Cory's room and borrowing some clothes, but I don't want to risk waking him up. Or questions. Definitely no questions about why I need clothes.

Shit, did I tell him how into him I was? God, I'm pretty sure I did, but I can't remember if he said anything back. Stupid watermelon mojitos. My head feels like it's been turned into a throbbing cotton ball.

I make my way down the stairs and creep down the hallway. Good so far, but I hear voices coming from the dining area and living room. After listening to assess the path of least resistance, I decide hustling past the dining room and out the back door is the best option.

I'm wrong.

"Yo, Spidey," Royer calls out, damn him. "You want some breakfast? We've got plenty."

I freeze in my tracks and turn slowly, holding my gloves in

front of my crotch and attempting a nonchalant air while facing down a crew of frat guys. It's an incredibly difficult feat in a spunk-stained spandex Spider-Man costume. Possibly more difficult than Calc 2. "Nah, I'm good, thanks. Just leaving. Very much leaving." I can't handle a bunch of bros right now, even friendly ones offering me breakfast—much less eggs and bacon. My stomach is queasy just thinking about it. Thank goodness my shift at Shenanigans isn't until later tonight.

"Shit, is that Cory's dude?"

For a split second, I feel a little twinge of pride in my chest. *Cory's dude.* I don't hate the sound of that. Does that mean he's mentioned me to his brothers?

"Goddammit, now we owe him dinner and drinks, and you know that asshole is gonna order the most expensive shit at Cosmo's."

"Huh?" That twinge of pride evaporates. Something is off, and I'm struggling to piece together what one of San Luco's fanciest eateries has to do with Cory and me.

"Oof, what, dude?" The guy who mentioned dinner and drinks scowls and rubs the bicep Royer just socked.

"Shut up."

"Why do you owe Cory?" I take the guys in, gaze searching each one as my pulse pounds and the pit in my stomach becomes an abyss.

"Shut the fuck up, Javi. Don't worry about it, man," Royer directs to me with a wavering smile. "It's nothing."

But Javi is still sitting there smirking like a chump, although I guess Royer's warning worked since he's not saying anything.

"Why do you owe Cory food and drinks at Cosmo's?" I press.

Royer darts another vicious look at Javi, and in the resounding silence, my brain comes online. Between the apology in Royer's gaze as he looks back at me, and Javi's smirk, I'm able to piece together the last couple of months with Cory, beginning to now. His insistence on sitting next to me in anthropology, disc golf, the invitations to the library, requesting my help with his costume. The afternoon out on his uncle's boat.

It's the last one that stings the most. I'm used to the occasional blush, to the heat in my cheeks, but for the first time since my mom got diagnosed, I feel the opposite. Every last tendril of warmth ebbs from my body, leaving me hollow and cold.

None of it was real.

I'm a fucking dare, or prank, or bet. A joke at the very least.

No, it's worse. I'm a late-nineties rom-com.

"I see," I say calmly into the tense silence, then do the only thing I can. Flee.

I BARREL PAST MY LaL ROOMIES IN THE KITCHEN AND THE LIVING ROOM, beelining for my room. Sensing someone behind me, I stop myself from slamming the door to my room shut and potentially breaking a nose. "Not right now, I need a minute." Or a decade. Never before have I wished so hard that I were Rip Van Winkle.

"Spence, what's going on?" Darby's voice drips with concern as she catches the edge of my door and slips in behind me before shutting it. "You disappeared last night. I was worried. You left your phone." She holds it up as I tear at my Spider-Man costume.

"Throw it in the trash."

She sits down on my bed instead, gaze flickering over me carefully. "Can I help?" She reaches for me, but I wave her off.

"I've got it. I'm fine. Just need to be alone."

She sighs. "No you don't. You love to air your grievances to me as much as I love to do the same. It's kind of our thing." She politely averts her eyes as I snap the spandex from my ankles and wing it toward the trash can. "Wow. Okay, this is going to be bad."

I pull on a pair of boxers. "My dumb ass told Cory that I liked him."

"Okay," she hedges. "But it's true. He seems like he likes you back, as much as I hate to admit something nice about a DIK. Did he ghost you or something?"

I shake my head, the lump in my throat enormous. "Worse. I was a joke. A bet. Something like that. I'm not sure."

Her expression darkens as I back up and start from the beginning of the night.

21

CORY

I woke up the first time to Spencer clambering out of bed and saying he was going to the restroom. Then I promptly fell back asleep.

I stir again later, rolling over to throw an arm around him and pull him closer, but there's just cool sheets and a small wet spot when I hitch my knee up in search of him. My eyes pop open, and I blink the sleep from them, squinting in the morning light.

Definitely no Spencer, and all his stuff is gone, too, the little sneak.

I ease upright, still gritty-eyed, and stare at the sheets. Did he... did I... no, that's definitely not pee. Did I have a wet dream? God, that would be hilarious irony. Or shit, did he?

This is too much mystery for a Saturday morning, and the only one I'm really interested in solving is why Spence isn't still here for me to curl around.

Maybe he was embarrassed about being so drunk last night? But he shouldn't be. I've seen worse. Hell, I've been worse.

I pick up my phone and fire off a text.

Cory: *Where'd you go? If you're getting all shy about being hammered last night, don't be. You're a cute drunk. And very amusing just like you said.*

I grin as I send it, thinking about how he dead-man sprawled in my bed last night, the hazy distance in his eyes, his drunken but earnest-sounding confession.

I liked taking care of him, and that's new for me, too. But I know I want more of it.

After five minutes and no reply, I decide he's probably gotten back to his room and passed out, so I slide from my bed, pull some gym shorts over my briefs, and head down to the dining room to see if there's any breakfast left.

I luck out with some scrambled eggs, a couple of scraggly strips of bacon, and a bagel that I carry with me into the common room, where Royer and some other brothers are sprawled across various pieces of furniture, presumably nursing their hangovers while watching highlights from the last Kings' football game.

"Dude," Royer says when I enter, then waves me closer. "Spencer—"

"I know, he was hammered last night. If he said anything rude, he didn't mean it." I plop onto the arm of his chair and scarf another piece of bacon, smiling at the memory of him lurching around indignantly. "He was just flipping about this internship, which is kinda my fault and—"

"Spencer's pissed, man."

I blink. "Pissed? Why?"

"He knows about the bet."

"The be—" I feel the color drain from my face to my toes. "What the fuck? That's not even a thing anymore. How does he know? Fuck." This is not good. Very not good. Why the hell did I even make that dumbass bet?

Royer's expression is apologetic. "I tried to stop it, Cory, but shit, you've never had anyone stay over, and the guys just assumed and caused kind of a ruckus about it when Spencer tried to sneak out this morning. I mean, they didn't say anything overtly, but Spencer's not an idiot. He figured it out or thinks he figured it out. Whatever he thinks he figured out pissed him the fuck off, and he bailed fast."

"Shit." I drag a hand down my face and then toss my plate onto Royer's lap, appetite gone in an instant. "I gotta go find him and talk to him. Explain it."

I can fix this. I know I can.

I TEXT SPENCER AGAIN AS I THROW ON A SHIRT.

Cory: *I need to talk to you.*

I see the bubbles pop up, then stall, then pop up again. Finally, they disappear without a reply.

I race out the door. Spencer's car is in his parking spot, but that doesn't necessarily mean he's there. The front entrance of the house is locked, so I knock and wait, skin buzzing with anxiety that beads my forehead with perspiration.

Darby swings the door open, a sour expression tugging her mouth into a frown. "Get out of here, jerk face. No, jerk face is too kind for a human garbage dumpster like you."

Yikes. Safe to say Spencer has told her.

She immediately tries to push the door closed again, but I throw up a hand to stop her. "It's not what you think."

She arches a skeptical brow. "So you weren't boasting to all your little frat bros you could get Spencer in bed or make him fall for you or whatever stupid games you assholes play in the name of that ridiculous scoreboard?"

"There's no scoreboard, I swear to god. I..." Goddammit. Why am I such an asshole? "Okay, that did happen at one point, I'll be honest, but that was just me being... that was just because..."

"You're a dick?" She starts to close the door again, but I keep the pressure on my palm to prevent it from budging.

"Yes, I'm a dick, okay? And yes, I made a dumb bet."

"So it *was* a bet."

"A dumb bet made offhand, and I wasn't thinking. That's not the case now—Darby, I'm into him, I want to be with him. So can you just let me in so I can talk to him and explain?"

She snorts out a derisive laugh. "Fat fucking chance. He doesn't want to see you anyway, and I'd like to say on his behalf, fuck you for humiliating him." This time, she throws her entire weight behind the door, and I don't resist when it slams shut in my face.

"There's not a stupid scoreboard!" I shout through it, as if that makes anything better.

I've really screwed up now. My shoulders sag under the weight of what's just happened and I sink against the doorway, gnawing on my lower lip as I try to decide what's next. I'm not sure I've ever screwed up this badly before, and gut instinct says there's no amount of charm or finesse that will get me out of the hot water I've plunged myself in.

I try another text to Spencer out of desperate optimism.

Cory: *I'm sorry. It's not what you think, and I'd really love the chance to try to explain.*

Just as before, there's no response. But unlike before, where I would probably pester him until he listened, that doesn't seem right this time. I'm the one who fucked up, and if he wants some space from me, he deserves it, even if it feels like it'll kill me. Maybe if I give him a little space, he'll cool down enough for me to explain.

"How'd it go?" Royer's gaze flickers over me as I return to the common room and flop down dejectedly.

"Don't even ask." I groan, throwing a hand over my eyes. "Jesus, I so royally fucked up. He won't speak to me and... and... god, I'm really into him, Royer. Like deep into him, beyond a stupid bet I made months ago. Until an hour ago, I was pretty sure he felt the same."

Royer rubs his jaw thoughtfully. "I've been in kinda the same sitch once. Royal fuckup. Back in middle school. With Darby, actually." He offers a wan smile when my head swerves in his direction.

"Did she forgive you?" Dumb question considering the last few weeks.

"Ehhh, I'm guessing not since she just texted me to 'get fucked' right before you came in." He blows out a breath that I echo glumly. "Soooo are you gonna give up or try and fix this?"

"He won't even talk to me, dude."

"I think I'm probably a lost cause where Darby's concerned, but I've got some ideas for you."

Spencer doesn't show up for anthro on Tuesday. I watch the space where he usually sits the entire time from my old spot at the back of the room near Royer, who's similarly miserable since Darby gave him the what for. I can't say I'm surprised he skipped class, but it's still disappointing. That's the one place I could logically see him without feeling like I'm invading his space. I'm even avoiding Shenanigans because I don't want to be overbearing. I mean, I do, I really fucking do, but I'm the one who screwed up.

Fortunately, there's other stuff going on to distract me for an hour or two. DIKcon is happening in a few weeks, and I join Royer and some of the other brothers in more presswork for that. I can tell Royer, like me, is seeking any and all distractions, and I'm pretty sure his squabbles with Jackson over decorations are purely to pass the time. We've sold a shit ton of tickets to the event, though—more than any other fundraiser we've held before—so I take some pride in that. That means we achieved our goal of reaching beyond just the Greek scene on campus. But it also inevitably leads me to thoughts of Spencer sitting across from me at Shenanigans, his eyes alight with excitement as we plotted the whole thing.

Is this how it's going to be now? Is every thought going to lead back to Spencer? I've not been in love with someone in—wait, shit. Am I in love with Spencer?

"Fuck." The word bolts out of me as I sit in the library that afternoon, pretending to study, not even looking studiously out the window this time because I'm too aware of the emptiness around me, the spot where Spencer usually sits beside me. Once again, no surprise, even though the optimist in me continues bringing Orange Sours in the hopes that he'll show up.

Someone shushes me, and it's enough to get me on my feet and out of there.

Back in my room at the DIK house, I stare out the window. Spencer's blinds are tightly closed, of course. And somehow I know that he hasn't been watching me, that he hasn't even looked once. The knowledge stirs an ache in my chest, and I rub it absently as I pick up the phone and thumb through my contacts until I get to my uncle's.

"Had a good time out on the Cat the other day, I assume?" He greets me with warm humor.

"Yeah," I say miserably at yet another reminder of how I've fucked up.

"So what's that sad-sack sound, then, kid?"

I smile thinly at the endearment. I've always found it weirdly comforting, and in a lot of ways, my uncle has almost felt more like an older brother I never had. "I was just thinking... You're on the committee that heads up that environmental policy internship here, right?"

"I am. Why, you interested? It's a little late, but you could apply next year. Christ, your mom would have a cow if you changed majors at this point, though. They're counting on you to take over the world. Or at least NYC." The last bit is tinged with a hint of sarcasm. He knows I don't want to go to NYC.

"I'm not changing majors. I have a friend, though. He had an interview the other day. Spencer."

The line remains quiet, so I elaborate. "Spencer Crowe—he's an ecology major. Junior. About my height, dark hair, piercing blue eyes. Great smile when you can get one out of him." Which I likely won't ever again.

"Ah yes, Spencer." My uncle pauses, which doesn't sound like a good sign. Shit, maybe Spencer wasn't being overdramatic after all. That makes me feel even worse.

"So did you all like him?" I prompt. "Are you going to pick him for the internship?"

"Technically, this isn't something I should be discussing with you." My uncle clears his throat and then sighs. "Spencer had great recs. Solid GPA, too. Easily one of our strongest candidates. But some of the others were equally proficient and interviewed better. Spencer seemed a little, ahhhh, discombobulated and maybe a bit unprepared. We found that surprising and a bit disappointing, given his application and qualifications."

My heart sinks. "That's my fault. He was with me on the boat. We stayed overnight, and I promised to have him back in plenty of time the next morning. I mean, I *so* would have. We had plenty of time, and he's been really stressed, but he was so relaxed on the water I didn't want to leave. We set alarms and everything, but his phone was beside mine, and I guess I turned his alarm off in my sleep and didn't even set mine right, because I'm a fucking idiot. Then the boat wouldn't start and..." I spill out the rest of the story on what feels like the world's longest exhale. "So he had barely enough time to get back to campus and get to the interview. I swear that's not him, though, Uncle Peter. He's the most diligent, fucking smartest guy I know, and he really deserves that internship. I promise. Is there another round of interviews? Could you bring him back in for a do-over or something?"

"We don't typically do anything like that unless there's an extenuating circumstance. Illness, death in the family."

"Please, I'm begging you. He would never be late. He works at Shenanigans on top of his full course load, and he's never late. He's never made below a B in anything. He's crazy smart and a great friend, and—" I've turned into a babbling idiot, and I don't even care.

"Is he your boyfriend?"

"No," I say glumly. "And not likely to be anymore, but that's my fault, just like him being flustered was, and I really, really wish you could give him another chance."

Uncle Peter is quiet for a long time, then says, "I can't make any promises, but I'll see what I can do."

"Thank you." Gratitude pours through me so fast it makes my eyes sting. "God, thank you so much. That's all I ask. It would mean so much to him and to me, even if he never speaks to me again."

"I sense there's more to this story but that maybe you don't want to tell me everything. Does he know you've reached out to me?"

"No, he's not even speaking to me, and I don't want him to know. It'll sound like I'm trying to... I don't know, be manipulative to get back in his good graces, and it's not that. I messed up, and I'm just trying to make at least part of it right."

It seems like the very least I can do.

22

SPENCER

I only skipped anthropology once before I decided I couldn't just avoid anywhere Cory might possibly show up forever. But what I can do is ignore him, which is the tactic I've taken for the past week. Fortunately—or luckily for him, rather—he's wise enough not to try to sit next to me.

I've been dreading every shift at Shenanigans, too, worried that he'll appear and I'll have to serve him, but he's been avoiding it, as well. I do give up tables with other DIKs to fellow servers when they come in. But I can't do that forever, either.

Tonight is decent so far, though. No DIKs in the last few hours, and we'll be shutting down soon, so I can breathe a sigh of relief even as a pang of longing sears through my chest. I tamp it down it angrily. Nothing was real, none of it. And therefore, the longing I feel isn't real, either. It's a symptom of a fantasy, of a stupid ploy, and I'm still an idiot, no matter the apologies Cory has sent and no matter what he's said. There's no way I can believe any of it.

Tell my heart that, though, because it stubbornly refuses to listen.

I drop another round of drinks off at a table full of sorority girls. Deltas, I gather, from one of their T-shirts. They've been great customers all night, so as I set their drinks down, I say, "Kitchen is about to close in case you all want anything else."

"We're good. Thanks, though," the one with a blonde ponytail says. Then she twists her mouth up, which I read as hesitation.

"You sure? The app trio is great for soaking up excess margaritas and future regrets." Wish I'd had some the other night before I went to Cory's frat house.

"I'm sure," the girl insists, but her mouth does that twisty thing again. She's had a few, so maybe she's just tipsy, but then she leans in and says, "I'm sorry, I'm kinda drunk, but I have to ask. You said your name is Spencer, right?"

"Yeah," I hedge. Fuck, did I screw up somewhere? "Do you need to talk to my manager about my amazing service?" I tease lightly, though I'm a little nervous. I can't say I've been on my game lately, after all, and it's totally possible I messed up an order or left them too long without refilling their waters. The last thing I need right now is to lose my job.

"No, not at all. I was just curious because..." She shoots a glance at her girlfriends, who are also looking at me intently now. "Are you the Spencer who totally turned Cory Ingram down?"

"Turned Cory..." I'm lost. Again. "Wait, what?"

"Yeah, my best friend, Laura, whose boyfriend is a DIK, was telling me this story about how Cory was trying really hard to get with this guy Spencer, and the dude totally shut him down and crushed him. Which is kinda funny because Cory usually gets whatever and whoever he wants. Anyway, no one knows who this Spencer guy is, and you're the only one I've ever met, so I'm curious." She narrows her eyes speculatively at me. "You're pretty hot. You probably get whoever you want, too. Are you, by chance, single?"

When she flutters her lashes at me, I choke on my own spit. After pounding my chest to recover, I say the only thing I can think to. "It wasn't me."

"Oh." She pouts prettily before her smile rights itself. "So are you single, then, and maybe straight?"

"Very much single, but very much not straight. Or bi." What a weird fucking night.

Things get weirder when I get home from my shift. After peeling off my clothes and washing the food smells off my body, I climb into bed and check my email, freezing on one in particular from Peter Bayliss, Cory's fucking uncle, with the subject line: Follow up interview.

Spencer,

The committee and I very much enjoyed meeting with you the other day. After some discussion and an overwhelming number of qualified and impressive candidates, we've decided to do a second round of interviews among our top five. You are part of that echelon. Please reach out to Mrs. Fairley within the next few days to schedule a second interview for next week that will work with your schedule.

Best regards,
Peter Bayliss

P.S. You might consider sticking closer to shore prior to your interview this time. But in the future, remind Cory that it's almost always a pinched or kinked line on that particular Cat. I'll get it properly fixed one day.

I reread the email three times, by turns overjoyed and increasingly suspicious, then hesitate over Cory's contact info, debating the wisdom of what I'm about to do. But the night has been too fucking strange.

Spencer: *Did you tell people I turned you down?*
Spencer: *And did you talk to your uncle about me?*

My phone rings immediately, and Cory's name pops up, causing my heart to seize in my chest. I close my eyes and take a fortifying breath, then answer.

"I don't think we should talk this way."

"God," Cory exhales. "It's so good to hear your voice."

It's so hard to hear his. "Did you hear what I said? I think we should just text. Two questions, two answers, that's it."

"Spencer, please. Just hear me out. Five minutes." There's a note of plea in his voice that I've never heard before, and even as angry as I am at him, it reaches through the red haze and softens me.

"Five minutes," I grant. "Then no more. I really don't want to speak to you again, and I don't like that you used your connection with your uncle to get me another interview, if that's what happened. I know I bombed it. I told you I did."

"I didn't. I mean, I did, sort of? Ugh. He wasn't supposed to say anything. I explained the situation to him and told him that it was my fault that you were late and flustered, that on any other day that wouldn't have happened—because I know it wouldn't have. So to me, that makes it an extenuating circumstance. I didn't beg him… much. Okay, maybe I did a little, but he told me he couldn't make any promises anyway. He said you were already a strong candidate. So if you want to be mad about that, fine, I get it, but Spencer, I was just trying to make things right. It was my fault. I told you I'd have you back in plenty of time, and I didn't."

"Right, but I could have told you I couldn't go in the first place. It was a stupid idea."

The silence stretches before Cory says wistfully, "Was it? I thought we had a really good time."

"In retrospect, it was a dumb idea, yes." That's all I'm willing to give him. "And what's this about you telling people I turned you down?"

There's another long pause, then, "Darby said I humiliated you, and I could see her point, so after I got back from very unsuccessfully trying to talk to you that morning—Darby is really good at barricading a door, by the way—I told the guys you turned me down outright, thinking that would make me sound like a dumbass. I also told them the whole thing bit me in the ass since I really like you. I said I didn't win you over or into my bed and that it was stupid in the first place. Which it was. Spencer, I'm so fucking sorry..." His voice cracks. "I was an idiot, an unthinking idiot, a total dick, and I definitely deserve your anger, but fuck... I miss you. I really fucking like you, and that's one hundred percent true. The night on the boat—"

"Was just more bullshit," I bite off angrily.

"No it wasn't, not for me. I stopped thinking about that stupid bet a long time ago. Shit, if I was still trying to do that, why wouldn't I have told them about the dressing room at the costume shop? Or any of the other times we hooked up, including the night on the boat? But I should have said the bet was off and was stupid in the first place, and I didn't. I let my pride and ego get in the way, and I just assumed nothing would come of it."

There's a lot to digest there, and I take my time doing it. So long that Cory speaks again. "Still there?"

"Sort of."

"Could you come to the window? Maybe open your blinds?"

"No, definitely not," I say, but I do, for the first time since everything happened. I edge closer to them and peek carefully through one of the messed-up slats. Cory is facing the window, looking at mine, though I'm certain he doesn't see me. He wears a forlorn expression on his face, his mouth drawn. A mournful pang rattles through me. I don't like that expression on him. As angry as I am… goddammit, I miss his smile.

"Okay," he says meekly, though he doesn't move away from the window. "I'm really sorry, again. If there's anything I can ever do to make it up to you, I'll gladly do it."

I gnaw on my lower lip, still studying him, and then shrug. "I forgive you. I don't want to talk to you now, or maybe ever again, but I forgive you." As much as I try, I still can't hate him. I don't think I ever did. "Good night, Cory."

He sighs. "Okay. Good night."

I toss my phone aside and drop onto the end of my bed, staring blankly at Ted as he swims around in his tank, the cories darting to and fro along the bottom.

I don't know what sucks worse right now. How much I miss Cory, too, or my fervent wish to sleep through the next two years.

But the latter isn't an option, and I have a new distraction now: nailing my second interview.

23

CORY

God, I dread anthropology now. I've returned to my former spot next to Royer in the back, which means I sit through the entire class trying to focus on the lecture but in reality sneaking glances at the back of Spencer's head and his little cowlick, wishing just one time he'd turn around and look at me.

But he never does. He's always first to leave, and I continue to give him space, even when it's the last thing I want to do. He was right. I struggle to accept when people don't like me, but I'm trying to get better about it. I can't sell myself to everyone; I just wish I hadn't done such a good job with him only to fuck it up. It's a bitter pill to swallow.

Royer nudges me as class lets out, but my gaze lingers on Spencer until he leaves the lecture hall. "Let's go grab something from the cafeteria," he suggests. "Or we could day drink." He's been as miserable as me since Darby shut him down, too.

"Can't. I need to run this business plan out to Jasper for his loan. Maybe dinner, though? As long as it's not at—"

"Shenanigans," Royer finishes for me with a wan smile. "I know. Fuck." He scrubs a hand over his face. "We have to snap out of this."

"Can't." I shrug. "I still don't get why Darby let you have it, though. You had nothing to do with anything."

"It's a trigger for her, I guess. She thinks I should have sternly reprimanded you from the get-go. She's probably right. I wasn't thinking. I feel like a shit friend."

"Nah, it's not your fault. It's all on me. I'm the idiot. Don't sweat it." I sock him lightly on the shoulder. "Meet at Shrimp Shack at seven?"

"Sounds good."

I head down to the marina next, a folder in the passenger seat. All I think about as I drive is Spencer. How the wind whipped his hair when he was sitting next to me, how the sunlight in his eyes made the blue of them almost translucent. I still can't believe how badly I messed up with the one guy in three years who turned me inside out.

I search the marina's parking lot for his car, knowing damn well it won't be there, and then make my way to the dock and sit on the end of it until Jasper's boat comes chugging toward the slip.

Paolo ribs me as usual, but my return fire is half-hearted as I help him with the lines and make idle conversation until Jasper appears.

Once he's sent the rest of the crew home, we drop into our usual spots on the deck, and Jasper commences our ritual of passing me a beer.

I trade him the folder for it and crack open the can, taking a long swallow before setting it aside. "I wrote up a business and marketing plan, along with a brief history and numbers based on the financials you gave me." I point them out on the spreadsheet I've printed for him. "It's not super in-depth, but I don't think it needs to be, according to the bank's website. They'll be doing their own research, too." He nods and flips a page as I continue. "Here's where I've laid out the goals for the business loan. I also had a friend of mine, Remy work up a new logo for you." I lean over and flip another page for him. "He's an art major who works at the tat parlor where I got my ink. Super talented."

"Damn, kid." Jasper flips back through all the papers, then resumes studying the logo. "This is something else."

I beam, pleased that he's happy, and he cuts a sidelong look at me.

"Can I pay you for all of this?"

"Hell no. I mean, you can pay Remy if you use his logo, but as for me... just let me come out with you a few times before I graduate and am gone foreverrrrrr." I sink back in my chair and take a long draught of beer with a sigh.

Jasper continues eyeing me. "Something's funny about you today."

"Eh." I tip my head back, considering the pink-gold glow of the clouds. "I screwed up something important, and I can't shake it off."

"A test? You can do better next time."

"No, worse. A person." I chuckle softly.

"My answer stands. You can do better next time."

"I don't think there will be a next time with him."

"Ah," Jasper grunts and is silent for a beat. "You're the advertising whiz here, but isn't there always another opportunity? Never known you as one to back down easily from something you want. Why start now?"

"I... I don't know. He wants me to leave him alone, I think, so I feel like I should respect that. I just wish I could get across to him how much he means to me."

Jasper thumps my knuckle affectionately. "Lemme say this again. You're the ad whiz. Aren't you supposed to be good at thinking outside the box?"

He's right, but my brain has been vacant of ideas for the last week, so I hum noncommittally and rise. "I'm gonna head. Let me know how the bank thing goes, okay? And if there's anything else I can do."

"Will do." Jasper nods with a grunt. "Got a big charter a couple of weekends from now if you want to hop on and crew."

"I might take you up on that." It'd be good to take a break from the party scene for a while.

"Hey," Jasper calls out as I hop onto the dock, and I cast another look over my shoulder. "If you don't want to go to NYC, tell your folks you don't want to. You don't have to please everyone all the time, you know. Who says you have to go to NYC to kick ass in the advertising world?"

The words arrow through my chest, an echo of Spencer that hits true.

"Yo," Javi calls out as I arrive back at the frat house. A bunch of guys are hanging out on the back patio drinking beer. Javi tosses me one as I close in.

I toss it right back to him. "I'm cool. Thanks, though." Usually, I'd join in, but I've got some things I need to do, and I want to be 100 percent sober.

Javi cocks his head and studies me for a long moment. "We're cool, right?"

Right after everything went down with Spencer, I might have had a slightly dramatic moment with Javi over his big mouth. Until I realized, once again, the blame really was all on me. Still, I've been a bit distant in general. That's not due to him, though.

"We're cool. Promise. I told you, it's all on me." In a way, it feels good to keep saying that aloud, to accept the blame for something I did, not try to justify it or convince myself or anyone else that I was misunderstood or just goofing around. I hurt someone, and I deserve the consequences of that, even if it sucks.

Once in my room, I close the door and lock it to avoid unwanted guests, then drop into my desk chair, staring at the contact I've pulled up on my phone for long moments before punching send.

"Hey, Sweetpea," my mom answers. Her voice is chipper, but I've noticed over the years a rushed quality to it. Like I'm always catching her in the middle of something. "Your dad is hosting a dinner or I'd get him on the line. How are things?"

This is the part where I usually fill her in on my classes, everything going on in the fraternity, the usual chitchat. "I made a B on my last communications test..." I start and then derail. I try to envision myself leaving California behind. My uncle, our house in San Diego—even if I'm usually the only one there—Jasper, the warm sunny days and the blue coastline, Spencer, even if he's no longer talking to me. "Actually, fuck it. Mom, I don't want to work in NYC after I graduate, and I don't want to intern there this summer. I want to stay in California."

"But—"

"I know New York is the better opportunity and our fastest-growing branch," I barrel on. "And I know you and Dad want me to ultimately run that branch and keep it all in the family, but I don't think I can. I don't know if I'm wired for that kind of 24/7 lifestyle or if I can do as good of a job as someone else can who really, really wants it." She's silent on the other end of the line, and I drop onto the end of my bed, then sprawl backward, like I'm weighted down by the disappointment I sense transmitting through the earpiece. *You would get used to New York and the lifestyle.* The same refrain I've told myself for months and months, pumping myself up by imagining stepping into a conference room, all eyes on me, envious glances and adulation, just like on campus. Now more than ever, it rings hollow when I compare it to the quieter comfort of time spent with Spencer or Jasper or my uncle. "You and Dad haven't taken time off in years, not even just for a weekend at home. The two of you have built a whole empire, but you never get to slow down and appreciate it. What's the point of having all this... this *stuff* if you never even get to use it? You don't have friends anymore, just work colleagues and clients. Last year, you took a flight to Minneapolis Christmas Day afternoon, and Dad flew to New York the next morning."

"Your father and I have been talking about that lately," she says with a sigh when I've finished. "About taking more time for ourselves. We argue too much over the business and never have downtime to reconnect."

"I know, and I don't want that. I want to be able to still meet up with my friends or, if and when I have a family or partner, spend time with them."

"Have you met someone? Is that what this is about?"

"No. I mean yes, I met someone, but it's over now," I confess. "He made me think deeper about a lot of things, though. I appreciate what I have, and I like working hard—I'm willing to work hard—but I don't want to spend the rest of my life just trying to accumulate more. God, I know that sounds ungrateful. Please don't think I'm ungrateful for all of the opportunities you and Dad have given me."

"No, sweetie," she says warmly. "It sounds smart, and self-aware, and mature."

I sit up. "Does that mean you're not upset?"

"It means I'm proud to have a son who knows what he wants, and if you don't want to go to New York, then we will find someone else."

I blow out an exhale that makes me feel twenty pounds lighter, and my mom chuckles.

"Were you afraid we'd disown you?"

"Nah, I don't know. It's just that you both worked so hard building the firm, it seemed like something I should want as much as you both did."

"Which confirms my suspicions that we got off track somewhere, put too much pressure on you, perhaps. A mother only ever wants happiness for her child, and however you want to write your destiny, I will always respect that it's your own." Her gentle tone wraps around me like a hug.

"Thank you." I rub the prickle in my chest and swallow the lump in my throat. "I miss you and Dad."

"I miss you, too, sweetheart. I'm going to talk to your father. What would you say to spending Christmas week in Telluride?"

"I'd say fuck yes, that sounds amazing."

"And if you have someone you'd like to bring along, you should."

Imagining Spencer in Telluride with me sets off that ache in my chest all over. If only.

THAT NIGHT, I LIE IN BED, ZONING OUT TO THE BLUE-GREEN projector light that reminds me of the ocean, its slowly shifting patterns calming. I scroll mindlessly through Instagram reels, then funny YouTube clips I've saved to cheer myself up. There are a few I wish I could share with Spencer, a thought that makes me smile wistfully. I miss him tremendously. Maybe sometime. Maybe sometime he'll forgive me. I wonder what it will take? Just time and space? Or is there something else I could do? Something else I could say? A last-ditch effort to show him how much I truly am into him, even if I started off as an idiot.

I saw at my lip as I eye the saved reels, and then I bolt upright.

I have an idea.

24

SPENCER

Darby is waiting for me when I exit the Life Sciences building Tuesday afternoon. "Soooooo?" She twiddles her fingers, expression hopeful. "Did you dazzle them?"

I smile, and it feels like the first genuine one I've had in weeks. "Dazzle is a strong word, but I didn't stutter or flail this time, and I think I made a good impression." I've spent the last week mentally rehashing my first interview and prepping for the next, going over my experience and coursework, thinking about my goals, until all of it rolled smoothly and confidently from my tongue. I know that this time I did the best that I could, and if they choose someone else, it's just not meant to be, the same as Cory. With effort, I push thoughts of him aside. He seems to creep into my consciousness constantly. "Want to go get lunch?"

"I thought you'd never ask. I'm starving." Darby links her elbow with mine, and we head to the dining hall, shuffle through the lines, and find a table near a window that overlooks one of FU's lush quads. It's another beautiful southern California day, and I don't blame Cory for not wanting to trade it for NYC. I wouldn't, either. I wonder if he gathered the courage to talk to his folks or if he ever will. Probably not.

There I go again thinking about him.

Darby's phone chimes with a message, and she stares at it for a long moment before tapping out a reply, then sets it aside and steeples her fingers, studying me. "Come to DIKcon with me."

"No," I say immediately. I squint at her. "Who just texted you?"

"Will. We've been messaging some."

"Will Royer, who you told in no uncertain terms to fuck off?"

"That's the one, yeah." She fiddles with a strand of her hair, looking guilty. I guess maybe she thinks I'll be mad, but I'm relieved.

"Good. You jumped the gun on that."

"I have a protective streak where you're concerned. I can't help it. Plus, the whole bet thing with Cory brought up all of those memories of Will and middle school, and I just reacted. But gah, he's apologized over and over again for that. He left a signed copy of *The Watchmen* at the house this morning. Right before everything went down, he helped me sew leaves to a Poison Ivy costume I'm working on, and I swear he was actually into it."

"He was into *you*." I squeeze her arm. "You don't have to build a case for him, I can tell. And I can tell you like him right back."

"But the whole Cory situation."

"Is on Cory, not Will."

"I can't believe I'm about to say this." She bites her lower lip, lungs expanding as she takes a deep breath and levels a piercing gaze upon me. "I think Cory really likes you, too. Will says he's miserable and feels like shit about everything."

"He should have thought of that before," I say, my rote reply.

"I know. He did a stupid, insensitive thing, but I think it really bit him in the ass, Spence."

"Good, he deserves that."

"He does, but..."

I frown. "I'm a big fan of butts, but I don't like the number of buts you keep tossing out."

She shrugs, deflating. "I just wonder if maybe he deserves another chance."

I laugh, thinking back to our conversation about Royer and the middle school dance. "Are you serious?"

"He's apologized a shit ton. He told anyone who would listen that you'd turned him down, which was another silly thing for him to do, but he was doing it from a place of... of... trying to make it right, I think."

"Maybe," I say noncommittally, even if what she's saying fills me with longing.

"Come to DIKcon with me—" She puts a finger up to silence me before I can protest. "Stop hiding. You don't have to forgive him. You don't even have to see him—it's going to be packed. And it's also going to be fun. You've done nothing but mope for the last few weeks, and you were really looking forward to this. I mean, jeez, the entire LaL house is going. Everyone I *know* is going. It was *your* idea in the first place. So come with me, hold your head high, and try to cut loose for a while. I'm telling you this as your best friend... You need it."

I suck on my lower lip, trying valiantly to deny the good points Darby makes.

"I just can't," I finally answer, and Darby leans her head on my shoulder with a quiet sigh.

"Okay, I get it. If you change your mind, though, we can go together."

Friday evening, I stand at the edge of my bed, staring down at the Dr. Strange costume I've laid out. For the past three days, I've waffled over attending DIKcon. Darby is right; I've fallen back into my previous trap of doing absolutely nothing but work, study, and sleep. I was looking forward to DIKcon, super pleased that the idea had taken wings, even before everything that had happened with Cory. I shouldn't be hiding, I tell myself, not even from him, no matter the cause. I'm an adult. And besides, anthro class is proof that I can ignore him in relatively close proximity and still function. Ish. And Darby's also right that it's going to be so packed anyway, I might not even see him. So why shouldn't I go and try to enjoy something I love?

I can do this.

I *should* do this. For myself, if nothing else.

I pull out my phone and text Darby.

Spencer: *I changed my mind. I'll go.*

I await a snarky reply, but what I get instead is a bunch of heart eyes and kiss emojis followed by, "Meet us downstairs at 7."

I take my time dressing. Dr. Strange wasn't my first choice, but I still feel a little embarrassed to show up as Spider-Man. As I dress, I gravitate toward the windows I've been resolutely avoiding.

Don't do it, I tell myself, then peer through one of the slats anyway, holding my breath. Cory's room is dark, but of course it is. He's probably already at the con helping set up. Still, the shadowed room fills me with a deep yearning that turns into a sigh as I exhale.

Once I'm finished dressing, I feed my fish, resting my forehead against the glass as I watch the cories dart about the bottom of the tank. Ted swims serenely back and forth in front of my eyes.

"I miss him," I say, the admission expanding that sense of longing in my chest, threatening to overpower me.

I straighten quickly, turn out my lights, and leave the room.

DIKcon is being held at an event center a half mile from campus. Darby and I walk alongside each other with the rest of our roomies, joining streams of other costumed folks trekking across campus. We spot a Shrek, a Groot, a Harley Quinn. People have seriously gone all out for this, more so than even Halloween, and Darby and I entertain ourselves by pointing out some of the more obscure cosplays.

Given the line stretching around the stucco building that looks like it was once a church, it takes us almost a half hour to gain entry.

"Damn, the DIKs went to great lengths to put on a proper con." Darby snickers at her own pun as we stare in awe. The DIKs must have teamed up with a bunch of art majors because there are giant wood panels dotting the cavernous space made to look like comic book panels, featuring various characters, along with painted set pieces from other movie and TV franchises. Gotham City, a landscape from *Guardians of the Galaxy*. There's even a TARDIS surrounded by people snapping selfies.

"One might say they're growers, not showers," I quip back with a tiny smile. It's truly impressive.

"Or growers *and* showers."

"Can you be both?" I ponder.

"Probably." Darby wraps an arm around me. "I'm just happy you're making a joke."

"Don't get used to it."

"Whomp whomp," she says, squeezing my waist, then squeals and points. "Oh my god, is that Edward Cullen?"

I follow her sightline to a guy I recognize vaguely as a DIK and who is covered, head to toe, in iridescent glitter. We cackle as he leaves a shimmery trail behind.

"Darby!"

We both turn at Royer's approach. He makes the perfect Geralt, down to the streaming white wig, only lacking the surly curl of the Witcher's lip because he's smiling too wide.

He throws his hands over his heart as he draws closer. "Goddamn, you look great." Darby preens, fluffing her skirt. She really does make a killer Maria Salazar. "You too, man." Royer flashes me a grin, the warmth in his voice catching me off guard. "I'm really glad you could make it."

"This is badass. Y'all did a great job," I tell him.

"Yeah, Co—" He winces. "I mean, we got hooked up by the art department. There's a whole comic shop, too." He points out a section of the room filled with racks of comic books and graphic novels, but I'm distracted, looking for Cory even though I told myself I wouldn't. There are more than a few versions of the Dark Knight milling around, but none of them are him.

I tune back in as Royer brushes a kiss over Darby's cheek. "I've gotta go make sure Darth and Luke are ready for their lightsaber fight, but I'll catch up with you after all the performances. Save me a dance?"

"Maybe," she says, her smile lingering as she watches him disappear into the crowd.

"God, you've got it bad." I roll my eyes at her, but it's halfhearted. I'm glad to see her happy.

"Shhh. Let's go get some drinks."

We make our way to one of the many bars scattered about, grab drinks, and spend the next half hour wandering through the con. Everyone is in a festive mood, oohing and ahhing over costumes, dancing in front of a large stage where a DJ booth has been set up.

At eight, the house music fades, and Royer's voice booms

over the mic. "Whassup, everyone? Welcome to DIKcon!" A cheer arises from the crowd, and Darby grabs my arm, pulling me closer to the stage where Royer is. A bunch of other DIKs stand behind him, and I suck in a steadying breath as I spot Cory among them, heart-wrenchingly gorgeous in his costume. I can't stop staring at him, thinking about his hands on me in the dressing room, his kiss, his muscles tensing beneath my touch.

Royer explains the history of DIK fundraisers, sharing the story of his brother's cystic fibrosis diagnosis. "When I got named social chair, I knew I wanted to do something a little different for our fall fundraiser this year, something that shows we're not just a bunch of exclusive DIKs. However, I can't take credit for this year's theme. That honor goes to Spencer Crowe. Spencer, where are ya?"

"Ohmigod," I hiss, snapping my gaze away from Cory as my cheeks flame. I try to duck, but Darby stops me, hissing back.

"You've got this."

I glance again at Cory, who now appears to be searching the crowd like Royer is.

Then I swallow and steel my spine. She's right: I've got this. I can handle this.

I lift my hand.

"There he is!" Royer booms. "Let's give Spencer a hand for his idea. Fun fact, Spencer also works at Shenanigans, so next time he's your server, how about tossing a coin to your server."

Darby groans at his *Witcher* joke, but I hardly hear her or the rest of what Royer says because Cory's gaze is on me, laser focused and penetrating, and it damn near takes my breath away. I forget the revelers around me, the boom of applause and whoops. The only thing I can see is the small, rueful smile that turns up the corners of his mouth and sets off an earthquake inside me.

It's not until Royer moves on, thanking others, that I come

back to myself and realize I'm smiling back. Like his, it's small and forlorn, but it's there.

"And just so you all don't think we just throw a bunch of kegs in a room and call it a party, we've even got a couple of performances, and we hope you'll stick around afterwards for the portion of the night we like to call 'let's all get shitfaced for a good cause.'"

The audience laughs, and Royer and the rest of the DIKs leave the stage, shortly replaced by a Darth Vader and Luke, who battle it out with lightsabers. It's obvious they put serious work into the choreography, which makes it all the more hilarious when it goes awry near the end and Darth's lightsaber snaps in half right before Luke nails him in the 'nads.

Next, a bunch of DIKs take the stage dressed as *Star Trek* characters and perform to a remix of the Firm's "Star Trekkin'."

"Oh god," Darby moans through her laughter. "That's a song that never should've been remixed."

"It's horrible," I agree with a laugh that grows as the DIK's dance becomes increasingly frenzied. It's wildly entertaining and objectively terrible, but god, it feels good to laugh again.

Darby pokes me. "Told you this would be fun."

She's right, but I refuse to give her the satisfaction of admitting it.

The Star Trekkers finish, and the stage goes dark for so long that Darby and I glance at each other, wondering if that's the end of the performances.

Then comes the sound of rain over the speakers. A spotlight flares cool white light on the stage as a guy in a suit and hat sashays across, twirling an umbrella to "Singin' in the Rain."

My eyes nearly bug out of my head. "Ohmigod," I hiss for the second time tonight. The gorgeous suited man is Cory. "Is he gonna…" Darby grins but doesn't speak, just tugs me closer and closer to the stage as "Singin' in the Rain" gives way to

Rihanna's "Umbrella," and a bunch of DIKs swarm the stage again.

Darth, Luke, Geralt, and the entire team of Star Trekkers fall into the synced steps of my most favorite recorded pick-me-up in existence.

My stomach flutters, and my pulse races as Cory steps behind a bunch of umbrellas before re-emerging in a French maid costume and dark bob wig, just like the video I vaguely remember mentioning when I was hammered in his room.

"Jesus Christ," I whisper as he moves toward the front of the stage and joins in the choreography. Around me, the revelers have burst into thunderous applause, many of them singing along as Cory executes the dance perfectly.

When the song reaches its bridge, he drops to his knees in front of me, gaze fastened to mine as he lip-synchs. It may be the cheesiest, sappiest thing I've ever seen in my life, and my heart doesn't give a single damn. It hammers in my chest, my breath coming fast as I stare back at him, bewildered, overwhelmed, amused, touched. And in love. Fuck, I'm in love with this silly DIK cosplaying a whole internet phenomenon for my benefit. He winks at me as he backs away for the finale, and the thunderous applause grows louder as the song ends and the stage goes dark.

I stand in stunned silence for long moments before turning to Darby. "Did you know about this?"

She shrugs mischievously. "He came up with the idea on his own, then ran it by me. I mighhhhht have said you'd like it. I told you, he really likes you. I think he might actually be in lo—"

I don't hear the rest of what she says because I'm pushing through the crowd, trying to get to the end of the stage, where all the DIKs disappeared. Royer spots me and grins, then points behind the curtain.

I rush through it, slipping between other DIKs, casting wild glances around until I spy Cory, tugging off the dark wig. Good god, he's even wearing the fishnets, and the sight of him makes it hard to breathe. When I touch his arm, he spins around, expression sobering with hesitation.

"Did you do that for me?" I blurt.

"I did, yeah." He offers me a cautious smile. "I was really hoping you'd come, but Darby said no guarantees, and then when I was doing it, it was really hard to read your expression. I couldn't tell if you liked it or—"

I smash my lips to the familiar warmth of his, cutting off the rest of his sentence. He opens to the kiss, one hand coasting up my side and coming to rest on the nape of my neck, keeping me close.

"I didn't like it," I gasp, and Cory rears back, worry shadowing his eyes. "I loved it. I fucking *loved* it and—"

"I love *you*," he murmurs. We both go still and wide-eyed, staring at each other. Then he breaks into a laugh. "That kinda slipped out, but it's true."

"I can't stop thinking about you. I think about you all the time. It's miserable. And electrifying."

"And terrifying." He nods.

"All of those things, and I love you, too," I confess, my lips brushing over his. "And I forgive you. I don't care about a stupid bet. We never would've gotten together otherwise, never would have spent all this time together. I would've continued to think you were just some dumb frat dude and not a guy who… who…"

"Is willing to don a French maid costume and lip-synch to Rihanna just to try to make you smile again?"

"Yeah, that." I'm buoyant and electric at once, my skin tingling and buzzing everywhere our bodies touch. "I missed you."

"Same. Did you look through my window?"

I shake my head. "Wouldn't let myself."

"I figured, but I kept hoping you would so you'd see my sad ass staring woefully in your direction."

I chuckle. "You have a thing with windows and staring out of them with variations of human expression, don't you."

"So do you." He bumps his forehead to mine. "Does this mean we can go back to our voyeuristic tendencies?"

"Yeah, as long as we can throw some overnights in the mix. And maybe an occasional boat trip."

"Disc golf?"

"Yes. And more library study sessions so I can judge your 'pondering the meaning of life' looks."

"I'll bring Orange Sours."

"Oh yeah, that's part of the whole deal. Where the hell do you get those, by the way? For real."

"I found the manufacturer. Turns out the company is a former client of my parents' firm. They have a brand manager who put me in touch with the manufacturing department. They're gradually phasing them out. Not big sellers, apparently, but they had stock on hand and were nice enough to offer to send me cases directly. I, ummm..." He rubs a hand over his jaw. "May have bought at least a three-month supply. Maybe more like two the way you go through them. Anyway, I've got the hookup so long as they keep producing them."

I gaze at him, and after a beat, he exhales a self-conscious chuckle. "Why are you looking at me like that?"

"I'm going to have to change your name in my phone."

"From Hot Idiot? *Finally.*" He barks out a laugh at my gaping expression. "Yeah, I saw that in the library once when you left your phone open on the messages. I figured the 'hot' part was a good sign, though." He mimics putting sunglasses on. "So what are you going to change it to?"

"Clever idiot?" I suggest with a smirk.

"May I suggest Sexiest Man Alive?"

"Easy there. I don't think you've seen the Bane out on the floor," I tease, but in all honesty, Cory *is* the sexiest man alive to me.

"How about just... 'my man.'" He licks his lips, and after a beat, we both break into loud laughter. "Way too cheesy, I know."

I nibble the side of his jaw. "But accurate."

25

CORY

I'm lighter than air for the rest of the night. I change back into my costume—with firm instructions from Spencer to reserve my "Umbrella" getup for future, more private venues—and we join the other revelers enjoying DIKcon. One drink and I'm able to get Spencer on the dance floor busting a move, and he's not half-bad. Every so often, I look at him and think, *This is only the beginning*, and a mellow warmth unfurls inside me.

I wonder if my former aversion to relationships was just because I hadn't found my person.

I had no idea it would come out of a stupid bet, though.

Spencer and I end the night on the moonlit sands of the beach across from campus, and we're not alone. It seems half of campus has the same idea, but we find a secluded place to settle, and I spread out my cape for us to sit on. Spencer slides out of his coat and pulls out his phone. "I need to check something real quick," he says, thumbing his screen to life. "Got a little distracted earlier."

"It was the fishnets, right?" I tease, and he grins and rolls his eyes.

"The fishnets didn't hurt, but... *holy shit*. Holy shit. I got it."

He thrusts his phone at me, and I skim the email from my uncle, breaking into a wide grin.

"I knew you would."

"Wait." He eyes me suspiciously. "You didn't..."

"I didn't do shit. I promise. God, talk about digging a deeper hole. You did that all on your own."

I pass the phone back to him, and he reads the email again, then tucks the phone away. He draws up his knees, folds his arms over them, and gazes sidelong at me, smile lingering as his shoulder nudges mine. "This has been an unexpectedly good night."

"Agreed." I kiss two fingers and lift them toward the sky. "Thank you, Tom Holland and Rihanna." As he chuckles, I scoot a little closer until our thighs align and mimic his posture, our heads close.

"Are you gonna start sitting next to me in anthro again?" He nuzzles my nose.

"Whoa, back up. You're taking things too fast now."

"Probably so. We'd better ease into it, go back to mutual masturbation at the window first."

"That makes way more sense." We both crack up, and when it ebbs, overtaken by the distant voices of other late-nighters and the lap of waves along the shoreline, I find his hand and slip mine into it. I've never held his hand before with such simple intent. His fingers are long and cool and feel really damn good intertwined with mine. "I told my parents I don't want to move to New York, that I want to stay in California."

Spencer lifts his head, surprise etched in his brows. "You did? What did they say?"

"I could tell my mom was disappointed. But she understood." I shrug. "And yeah, maybe I won't advance as quickly here. Or even ever, but I'm good with that. Just being another guy at the firm sounds pretty nice."

"Will you still intern with them this summer?"

"Yeah, but at the San Diego office." I poke his arm. "You know, GlobalWatch has summer internships for students there. Just saying." In addition to our family home, my parents have a downtown loft in San Diego, and I can't help but imagine me and Spencer there together. Maybe I'm getting a little ahead of myself, but the way Spencer's smile blooms is promising.

"Funny, I'd already planned to apply for it in the spring." Spencer's gaze locks on mine, his eyes going solemn and intent. "I don't really have much experience with relationships. I've hooked up, yeah, and I dated a guy freshman year of high school, which basically consisted of us kissing a lot and rubbing against each other before he decided he had a crush on someone else. Then my mom's diagnosis, and… it just wasn't ever a priority."

I run a finger along his jawline. "Lucky for you, you're in the presence of a relationship expert." We both crack up, but when I sober, I meet his eyes again, hoping he can read the sincerity within them. "We'll figure it out our own way. The way I see it, haven't we already been doing the things most couples do? Hanging out, making out, flirting."

"I've never flirted with you. You're the flirt."

"Bullshit." I knock my knee against his, and he careens sideways, catching himself on the palm of his hand with a chuckle. "You started it with that dumb nacho joke."

"That wasn't flirting," Spencer protests, then tilts his head pensively. "Okay, maybe it was. Just a little. I can't believe I'm admitting that." He dusts the sand from his palm. "So what would boyfriends do next, do you think?"

I pretend like I'm giving it serious thought. "Sex. Lots of sex."

He grins and rolls upright, snagging his coat from the ground before extending his hand to me. "That's the best idea you've had all night."

"Better than 'Umbrella'?"

"Fair point." He laughs. "Second best idea. Let's go to my place."

I shake the sand from my cape, and we start back toward campus, arms wrapped around each other. I soak in the comfort of Spencer's presence, the fit of his lean form against mine, and from the way he melts against my side, he seems to be doing the same.

As we near the softly glowing windows of the LaL house, I dip closer and nuzzle the side of his neck, inhaling the scent of his skin, the quiet moan he lets out. "Have you ever been to Telluride?" I'm pretty sure I know the answer.

It takes him a second to reply with a breathy, distracted "No, but I've always wanted to go."

EPILOGUE
SPENCER

A year and some change later

Cory's uncle is at Luco Landing, hosing off the side of the *Gaia* when we arrive on a brilliantly blue afternoon in early March. Cory and I wave as we approach, and I take over hauling our wheeled cooler so the pair can exchange a hug.

"I've got her all gassed up for you." Peter turns off the hose and wipes his hands on the thighs of his shorts. "Took her for an early morning run. No pinches in the fuel line."

"Sweet." Cory grins as he hops on deck. "Thanks."

Uncle Peter winks at me as he extends his hand, our shake turning into a quick but affectionate back clap. "Congratulations on UCSD, Spencer. Not that I'm surprised."

"Thank you, sir, and thanks again for the recommendation." Peter and I had hit it off during my environmental policy internship at FU, which had led to a summer internship at GlobalWatch, and played a huge role in my deciding to pursue a Master's in Public Policy at UCSD. I'd just gotten the acceptance letter yesterday. When Cory insisted we spend today celebrating, I didn't mount even the slightest protest. I've been on pins and needles for the last couple of months, waiting to see if I got in, and I'm pretty sure every cell in my body exhaled when I opened the envelope and saw "Congratulations."

"It was one of the easiest recommendations I've ever written."

"Now you're just flattering him," Cory teases.

"Is there anyone in your family who isn't charming?"

Peter chuckles, but it's a fair question. I swear every blood relation of Cory's that I've met is as affable and socially magnetic as him.

"Probably a reclusive cousin somewhere in the family tree, who knows." Cory reaches for the cooler as I hand it over to him, then addresses Peter. "Sure you don't want to come with us?"

"Nah. I've got things to do." Peter's silver brow crinkles. "I thought there were supposed to be more of you?"

I roll my eyes. "Darby and Royer got 'caught up' in something."

"Sheets, probably." Cory cackles, and Peter shakes his head. Royer and Darby have come out with us on the catamaran a couple of times, but Darby struggles with getting seasick. I don't blame her for staying behind. And besides, it's kind of nice to have Cory all to myself. I had shifts at Shenanigans all weekend, and as VP of DIK house, Cory had to be at their mixer Friday night. I crashed in his room after my shift, but alone time with bass thumping the walls isn't the same thing as the open air and the sea.

After Peter leaves, I untie the lines and toss them to Cory before hopping on board. Cory glances over at me from the helm as he cranks the boat. "Wanna guide her out? It's sturdy, I promise."

It took me a month after Cory and I officially got together before I'd even touch the wheel of the catamaran, afraid Murphy's Law would strike the second I rested a hand on it and the boat would sink immediately. Cory still loves to tease me about this. It took me another six months after I got my boating license before I'd captain the catamaran without Cory within arm's length of me in case anything went wrong.

I take the wheel and steer us toward the mouth of the marina as Cory bustles about, tidying the lines and prepping to hoist the mainsail. I sneak glances over at him as he moves. His tight ass, the bunching muscles of his calves, the knowing look he aims at me when he catches me looking. I still can't believe he's mine sometimes.

Once we're on the open water, he rejoins me, cracking a soda that he passes to me to share before fixing me with a wicked grin that I don't trust at all—even if I love being the recipient of it. We spent the rest of junior year and all summer at his parents' San Diego loft basically fucking our way through the days and exploring the city in the downtime. Even a year later, I've still not gotten sick of that grin, despite how it used to torment me.

For two people who were uncertain about how a relationship was supposed to work, we seem to be managing just fine.

"I think you should dock the boat when we come back," Cory says.

Ah, so that was the source of the gleam in his eyes. "Nope, not a chance. I'm not ready for that yet."

"I think you are. Plus, the buoys are there for a reason." He nudges my foot with his. "C'mon, it's time to expand those seafaring horizons. Don't you want to dazzle your parents when they get here?"

"I don't want to embarrass them by taking out an entire marina with a half-a-million-dollar catamaran," I counter. My parents' California trip is something Cory and I cooked up after he came home with me for Thanksgiving and learned my parents hadn't ever been outside of Texas except when we originally drove to FU my freshman year. They, like Cory's parents, are people who rarely have time to relax. Just for different reasons. So instead of partying it up during spring break, Cory and me, my parents, and his are going to tour the coast of California in Ingram style. It'll be the first time they all meet, and I'm nervous as heck about it, but I've also spent enough time with Cory's parents to appreciate their hospitable, if gregarious, tendencies. Deep down, I know they'll all get along.

But I don't want to sink a boat or a marina.

I set my jaw and shake my head. "Maybe next time they come visit."

"Mmm. I like the sound of that: next time. Then tonight, you'll just practice." Cory sidles behind me, wrapping his arms around my waist and brushing his lips over the nape of my neck until I groan. He knows every one of my weak spots. "Say yes."

"That's coercion."

"I know." He's totally unrepentant, and now my dick is getting hard. It's a combo I've gotten used to. "Just try. For me?"

If I turned around, he'd fix me with that dark-eyed plea he knows I struggle to resist. This is what it's like to date a charming-ass man. Most of the time, I don't hate it. "The last time you told me to try something for you, I ended up in fishnets."

"And I ended up with cum all over my chest."

"I didn't hear you complaining."

"Because your cock was in my mouth."

"Won't be the last time." That had been a good one, though. We've managed to sneak in a couple of cons and cosplay meet-ups here and there. It's not Cory's thing the way it is mine, but he loves the people-watching, and he loves how our nights end when we're both decked out. Works for me. Likewise, I've taken up disc golf and play with him and Royer whenever I can, though he kicks my ass almost every time.

The wind catches the sail, speeding us over the water, and exhilaration hits, making me light-headed and content as I tip my head back into the rush of air. Cory keeps an arm around me, his chin on my shoulder, his gaze on the play of light over the water.

A HALF HOUR LATER, WE DROP ANCHOR, THE SHORE A DISTANT LINE that shifts with the bob of the boat. We carry the cooler up to the front deck and devour sandwiches I grabbed from Shenanigans before Cory hands me an ice-cold beer and toasts me when we crack it. "To UCSD."

"To being gainfully employed at one of the hottest advertising firms in the country," I return, and he cracks up.

"That's hardly as impressive as getting into a master's program."

"It's impressive to me." Cory had a couple of months where he considered changing his major before going ahead with his summer internship at the firm in San Diego, then ended up loving it there. Enough that he figured out it truly wasn't advertising he hated, just the idea of leaving California anytime soon. With that resolved, he leaned wholeheartedly into taking a position in SD as a brand strategist upon graduation.

"Hang on, there's something else." Cory hops up, vanishing along the side of the boat and returning shortly with a plain brown box. "Don't get too excited, and fair warning, it's kinda cheesy, but I thought you deserved a gift."

Before Cory, and considering the lack of relationship experience, I'd never really received gifts, but it's something I've discovered I love, and I do the same in return. Usually, they're just small things here and there—a blue-green light like the one in his room at the DIK house from him, a silly ornament for his rearview mirror from me to replace the original stuffed emoji that's become kind of a thing for us. Every so often, I'll change them out and see how long it takes him to notice it.

I grin and steal a kiss. "This better not be a Fleshlight," I tease.

"Pffft. We're each other's Fleshlights. Open it."

I unseal the box and pull out a folded T-shirt on top of paper stuffing. Blazoned across the front is the UCSD logo.

"Your first official tee. I wanted to get to it before your parents did because I'm competitive like that." He grins rakishly, and I crack up as I hold it over my chest.

"It's perfect. Thank you."

"Keep going."

I dig through the stuffing until I encounter something hard and pull it out gingerly.

"It's for Ted and the cories," he explains.

I turn the little green Jeep in the light. It's a near perfect replica of Cory's. "I fucking love it," I say, with undisguised appreciation.

"Darby hooked me up with one of her 3D design friends." He ducks his head, peering at me sidelong. "I told you it was silly."

"Shut your mouth. Ted and the cories will be swimming in style now. And every time I look at the tank, I'll be reminded of—"

"The fateful day I stole your parking spot. Aka, the best day of your life."

We both crack up, and I lean in, tasting the laughter on his lips before placing the Jeep and T-shirt back in the box and resting back on my palms. "What a nice fucking day."

Cory leans back, too, his fingers resting lightly on top of mine. "The little things, right?"

"The little things, yeah. Like the wind in your hair. Sandwiches. A big-ass catamaran."

"Speaking of," he says slyly. "You ever been blown on the deck of a big-ass catamaran?"

I cut a look at him sidelong, trying to ignore the way my cock twitches with interest in my shorts. "I don't think we've ever done that before." I glance around. "But... right here in the open?" We're in plain view.

"Sure, why not?"

"People." I gesture as a speedboat passes by. There's another cruiser on our left, too. "Can you be arrested on the water for public indecency?" I ponder, even though my burgeoning erection says I'm already sold on the idea.

"No one will see." He waggles his brows.

"They might. It's risky, even for you." I feign skepticism. "Bet you you won't."

His brow hikes up, mischief returning to his eyes. "Bet you I will," he says, the words murmured along my jaw as he palms my crotch and works my zipper lower.

"You win." I groan as he squeezes my hardening cock. I cave easily where Cory is concerned. I think I always will.

"So do you." He slides between my thighs, his fingers deftly pulling my button through the hole and my zipper all the way down. He looks up at me, that damn irresistible glint in his eye. "I've been thinking about this since we got on the boat." His hands slip behind the waistband of my briefs, and he doesn't wait for a reply before sinking lower. With the first breath of warm air against my cock, I'm putty.

"Fuck," I murmur, voice hitching as he closes his mouth around me. Heat rushes up my spine and colors my face as he caresses the sensitive spot on the underside of my cock with his tongue. I bury my fingers in his hair, guiding him as he starts to bob his head. His eyes lock on mine, something deep and intense in their brown depths, and the temperature in my veins shoots up again, my heart stuttering and my breath catching. I stare down at his mouth, his lashes and lips, memorizing this moment.

I want to go slow, want to make this last, but the man is too damn talented. And also apparently on a mission to make me lose it. My hips jerk, my thighs flex, and before I know it, I'm spilling down his throat and crying out as pleasure crashes through me.

I fall back to my elbows, gasping, and Cory crawls up my body. He threads both hands through my hair, kissing me hard and deep.

"How was that?" His voice is husky as he kisses his way to my ear, his still-hard cock pressing against my thigh.

"Let's just say it was a bet well worth losing." When I unbutton his shorts, he pushes into the grip of my hand, cock thick and hot.

He braces on one elbow above me, shoving his shorts lower before his hips dip, his cock gliding along my softening one. "Goddamn," he whispers, picking up the pace, and I collapse fully backward, one hand on his hip, urging him faster, the other closing over our dicks. Cory's eyes flutter at the additional friction, and before I can tell him to fuck me, he moans a curse, his load spattering hot all over my abdomen.

"Jeez, you really do have a thing for exhibitionism," I tease fondly when he rolls off me, panting.

His head lolls in my direction, a loose, sated smile on his lips. "This isn't new information."

I just like to remind him. In the intervening silence where we both catch our breath, I think back on previous adventures. All the window sessions we've had. The library once. His Jeep. Holy shit, the number of times we've messed around in his Jeep, just because. I'm pretty sure I'm as ruined for life as his Jeep's interior. The thought makes me chuckle, and when he asks what I'm laughing at, I tell him, and he joins in until we're breathless all over again.

Finally, we get it together, and he ticks his chin at the mess on my stomach. "Should we take a swim to clean off?"

"Are sharks attracted to semen?" That sets off more laughter. "Who are you texting?" I ask when Cory reaches for his phone and taps out a quick message. He holds up a finger so I'll wait, then turns the screen toward me with a grin when the reply comes, three quick pings in a row.

Cory: Are sharks attracted to semen?
Darby: ...
Darby: I'm suddenly not regretting staying on campus now.
Darby: For the record, no. But I know you already knew that, you idiot.

He sighs happily. "Messing with her never gets old."

WE TAKE A CHILLY SWIM IN THE PACIFIC AND HEAD BACK TO SHORE after the sun has sunk below the horizon. Warm air buffets us as we drive back to campus, and I tilt my head back in the passenger seat like I always do, closing my eyes, a smile playing over my lips as I soak in the atmosphere, the perfect day, the gorgeous man I love and who loves me back.

"I love you," I murmur, opening my eyes again as the car slows near the parking lots of our respective houses.

"You're welcome." He chuckles and steals a kiss as I lightly slug his bicep. "I love you, too, Spencer Crowe," he replies, then inclines his chin toward the full parking lot. There's not a free space to be seen. "Any suggestions on how to solve this parking conundrum? Should I just go park by the dumpster on Lee?"

"Or you could just park behind me."

"Double-parking? The scandal." Cory feigns shock, palms slapping lightly against his stubbled cheeks. "Sure you won't yell at me for blocking you in?"

"Nope, I'll just nudge you awake if I need you to move it."

He laughs and eases the Jeep behind my car. "Guess that means I'm sleeping at your place tonight."

"You bet."

Thanks so much for reading Bet You! If you're curious about Chris and Aiden, make sure to grab their story, The Glow Up!

Want more from me? For more college guys getting it on, check out Want Me. And to keep up with my new releases, come join my Facebook group, Wilder's Wild Ones.

MEET ALL THE COUPLES OF FRANKLIN U!

Brax and Ty's story:
Playing Games

Marshall and Felix's story:
The Dating Disaster

Charlie and Liam's story:
Mr. Romance

Spencer and Cory's story:
Bet You

Chris and Aiden's story:
The Glow Up

Cobey and Vincent's story:
Learning Curve

Alex and Remy's story:
Making Waves

Peyton and Levi's story:
Football Royalty

MORE BY NEVE WILDER

Rhythm of Love Series

(Contemporary Romance, audiobooks available)

Dedicated

Bend (Novella)

Resonance

Extracurricular Activities Series

(New adult/college, audiobooks available)

Want Me

Try Me

Show Me

Playing For Keeps Series

(Sports romance, co-written with Riley Hart, audiobooks available)

Rookie Move

Wages of Sin Series

(Romantic action adventure and suspense, co-written with Only James, audiobooks available)

Bad Habits

Play Dirty

Head Games

Nook Island Series

(Contemporary Romance)

Center of Gravity

Sightlines (Novella)

Ace's Wild Series

(Multi-author series)

Reunion (Novella)

ABOUT NEVE WILDER

Neve Wilder lives in the South, where the summers are hot and the winters are...sometimes cold.

She reads promiscuously, across multiple genres, but her favorite stories always contain an element of romance. Incidentally, this is also what she likes to write. Slow-burners with delicious tension? Yes. Whiplash-inducing page-turners, also yes. Down and dirty scorchers? Yes. And every flavor in between.

She believes David Bowie was the sexiest musician to ever live, and she's always game to nerd out on anything from music to writing.

And finally, she believes that love conquers all. Except the heat index in July. Nothing can conquer that bastard.

Join her for daily shenanigans in her FB group:
Wilder's Wild Ones

facebook.com/nevewilderwrites
instagram.com/nevewilder
bookbub.com/authors/neve-wilder
amazon.com/author/nevewilder

ACKNOWLEDGMENTS

I owe a lot of people a debt of gratitude for helping this book come to life. It started with May Archer, who helped me brainstorm the heck out of Cory and Spencer's premise. Kelly Fox, who patiently listened to me spill my jumbled thoughts on the characters and, with her usual insight, helped me nail them down. Caroline Decherd, who did a "temperature check" on the first several chapters and assured me it wasn't half-baked. To Riley Hart for constant and kind encouragement, and for inviting me to be a part of this project in the first place. Janine Cloud, who reads my first drafts and isn't afraid to tell me when I've written the worst sentence she's ever read. Sandra Dee fixes my grammar fails. Thank you to Charity VanHuss for proofing and to my amazing PA, CC Belle, who makes my job infinitely easier in a multitude of ways. And finally, thank you to my reader group, Wilder's Wild Ones. The support I've received from y'all over the years is a huge part of what keeps me going.